William Chambers Bartlett

An idyl of war-times

William Chambers Bartlett

An idyl of war-times

ISBN/EAN: 9783743304918

Manufactured in Europe, USA, Canada, Australia, Japa

Cover: Foto ©Andreas Hilbeck / pixelio.de

Manufactured and distributed by brebook publishing software
(www.brebook.com)

William Chambers Bartlett

An idyl of war-times

AN IDYL

OF

WAR-TIMES.

BY

Major W. C. Bartlett, U.S.A.

―――――――

NEW YORK CITY:

LEW VANDERPOOLE PUBLISHING COMPANY,

1890.

COMPOSITION, ELECTROTYPING AND PRESSWORK
BY W. M. HALSTED, 33-43 GOLD STREET, NEW YORK.

AN IDYL OF WAR-TIMES.

CHAPTER I.

It was a cold, clear night of February, 186–, years before the tide of that migratory spirit which obeyed the behest of fashion and interest, had obliterated the old familiar landmarks of lower New York, and established farther inland, upon bases of grander display, the alluring temples of Bacchus and Terpsichore. To one unfamiliar with the political history of the times, before whose eyes the moving panorama of opposing hosts had never passed ; upon whose ears had fallen no other sounds than those evolved in the busy life of a mammoth city—the every-day existence of New York would have contained no suggestion at variance with a preconceived idea of a populous and opulent metropolis. Though the exigencies of the great civil war had for two years been tugging at

the resources of men and money which,
open-handed, had been placed to the Nation's
credit, it would have taken an eye more crit-
ical than that of a novice, to detect any gap
in the living wall of humanity which crowded
the streets by day, and swelled the tide flow-
ing into restaurant or theatre at night. And
yet, responding to that clarion note, which
had through city and country town—through
the busy marts of trade and the peaceful fields
of husbandry, proclaimed their country's
need, thousands upon thousands of voices had
answered—" Here!"—the places which had
known them, knew them no more ; their foot-
steps were pressed upon unwelcoming
ground; side by side, shoulder to shoulder,
middle age and youth, country born and city
bred, in espousal of a common cause, animated with the same desire, had dropped
plough-share and pen, pruning-hook and
ledger and filled the ranks of a grand fra-
ternity.

" Charity," seated upon her graceful throne
bathed in the reflected light of her own bene-
ficence, crowned with the dual blessing of

bestowal and of gratitude, was upon this
night of February, putting forth her hand
again in aid of the suffering wives and children, whom the cruelties of war had left widowed and fatherless. The "Academy of
Music," whose walls might tell the tale of
many a triumph; whose spaces from pit to
proscenium, teem with association; where
genius has received its baptism of immortality and munificence in the garb of Revel, dispensed a royal charity, was to be thrown open
for a crowning effort. "Delmonico's" was
a scene of light and animation, as, at an early
hour of this evening, two gentlemen seated
themselves at a cozy table, in a corner looking out upon the avenue. Both of them
were army men and one carried, and would
carry to his grave a scar of honorable
warfare. Above the average height of men,
with a faultless figure, and a face singularly
handsome, Charlie Blaisdel might have married almost any girl for the asking. He had
wealth, talent, a chivalric manner of address
—nearly every quality to please a woman,
except constancy. He had thought himself

in love a dozen times, and had discovered in
the light of some new attraction that his supposed ideal had taken wings, with promise of
materialization in the latest acquisition to his
lengthening list of fair divinities.   Hugh
Griswold, his companion, was a man himself,
possessed of form and features which classed
him among the handsome men of his day.
Straight as an arrow, a soldier in all his bearing ; modest, almost to timidity ; a born lead-
er of men, and with an estimate of woman
which took its richest coloring from the almost idolatrous love he bore his only sister
and widowed mother; he was not a man to
confuse a transient fancy with the passion of
a life, and never, till a year before, when
sickness had brought him home, and, amidst
his wanderings among the mountains seeking
to hasten a lagging convalescence, the pathway of pretty Kitty Wilmerding crossed his
own, had he known the potent charm which
lay within the hollow of a woman's hand, or
the glad surprise which followed in the foot-
steps of enthrallment.   But Kitty had awakened him out of his dreamless sleep, how, he

never could understand, any more than many another to whom the revelation of an absorbing passion comes quick as a lightning flash; its work accomplished before the senses have recovered from the shock. Certain it was, that when he awakened, one bright morning, he made a discovery which turned the current of his thoughts toward a distant goal, hitherto unknown and unsuspected.

Hugh Griswold was not a man to temporize. If there was a duty before him he gave his whole energy to its fulfilment; if on pleasure bent, he was gay as the rest—fertile in device, hearty in co-operation. But he suddenly found himself upon a strange pathway —very beautiful were its surroundings, indeed, but it was an avenue he had never trodden; and whither would it lead? "That is just what I shall find out," was his mental resolve, and he saw no reason to swerve, any more than when at Fredericksburg, his battery had been ordered to a point where he *knew* the fight would be hopeless and unequal. If the matter now in hand was not a positive duty, it was akin to it, for what right had he,

he reasoned, to love a girl and she be none
the wiser of his thought of her? With his
strict notions of right and wrong, such a
course would be insult to her. He could
not carry about with him in his heart, the
image of a girl who had given him no patent
of hope at least, and beside, it was unsatisfactory to him, and so in his straightforward
way, he had asked Kitty as they were riding
together the day before he took leave of the
autumn-tinted hills, and had reined in to ad-
mire a distant feature of the landscape,
if she would be his wife. "He would ever,"
he said, "associate the memories of this visit
with her. Could he not carry back with him
the *hope* at least, that some day she would be
to him more than a memory?" But Kitty
was young and had admirers by the score,
and some very tender words Charlie Blaisdel had spoken to her of late, chiming in as
they did with other rhythmic cadences of her
happy life, made her loath to still the pleasant
poetic jingle by a surrender to dull realities;
she wanted unbounded space to breathe in;
the world for a playground, (for a while, at

least), and then, what if she *did* bestow herself upon this man, and the fortunes of war took him from her forever, and she were left widowed, even before her wedding-day—oh! the thought of it was too horrible to bear, and so, not to cast him off, not to kill the hope he had uttered, or within herself that germ which, because of her sincere respect and liking for him, she knew might ripen into all that he could ask of love and faithfulness, she bade him wait, and he, in the nobility of his soul, recognized the trouble of her spirit, and pressed her no more, only, upon leaving her the following day, he had said : " You bade me wait, and that has kindled within me the gleam of hope for which I sought. I have much to thank you for in the pleasure of the past few days. I shall have much more, if my waiting meet with its coveted reward."

And now Hugh has returned to New York for a couple of days, before starting with his battery for the west, and meeting Charlie Blaisdel, they had dropped in at Delmonico's to dine together.

" Of course, Hugh, you'll go to the

'Charity' to-night—splendid luck getting here in time; it's always the swell thing of the season, but to-night, they say, will eclipse any previous efforts." "I hardly think so," answered Griswold. "I have no ticket and to-morrow I have much to do." "Doesn't matter," retorted Blaisdel, "about the ticket, I'll arrange that, and you *must* go; why, everybody will be there, and such an array of beautiful women. Why, man, do the gods provide such feasts for such as *we* to turn our backs upon? Of course, you'll go, if you have to transact your business to-morrow in your dress suit." "All right, then, I suppose I must," answered Griswold. "I'll straggle in some time during the night, but, you know, dancing is not much in my line." "Oh, you don't have to dance if you don't care to, the boxes hold the special at-tractions, and that is my idea of bliss; a blaze of light; the loveliest music in the world; and a corner of a box with your divinity. Ah! Hugh, I came near losing all that, when that confounded bullet made its round my way." "You're loved of women more than of the gods, Charlie, I suspect, and so not predestined to an early grave," said Hugh.

Blaisdel raised his glass to catch the sparkle of the amber-colored liquid, as the light from a chandelier overhead fell into it, and bowed in mute recognition of the compliment. "You know I do not go back to the field, I suppose," he said, presently.

"No? Well, you've paid full tribute to Mars, I should say, with your record and that wound. What do you hope to do with yourself?" asked Griswold. "Take to the law, I suppose. I've broken so many of them myself I ought to be a good pleader for others." "Gaining your clients on the 'experto crede' principle, I presume," laughed Griswold.

"Perhaps so, if ever I get any, but I shall not be dependent upon my practice for my bread," said Blaisdel; "a revered uncle, peace to his ashes, probably foresaw my necessities, and provided for them, but *something* I must do; a man cannot stay at home in these times and be idle." "I should fancy not," said Griswold, "still, I almost envy you a sojourn in New York. Look where you will, New York is always in the lead." "Yes," answered Blaisdel, " but even the gayeties of this great metropolis pall after a time, and I'm not so sure but that the man to whom pleasure comes only in the intervals of hard work is not the happier. Give a man an aim in life, stimulate his ambition in whatever direction you like, set a goal for him, however distant, and every energy of his being becomes aroused—that man sees every phase of life, it is no one-sided picture to him, it's a hard field to fight and conquer. Very many do not conquer, you may say. True, but they fall in the full rush and glory of the charge, fall while the blood is up, and they are filled with a noble purpose. *Fate* may be against them, but for *such* men there is the *Destiny* of immortality." ' I never supposed you so inspired, Charlie," said Griswold, " but I think you are right—the only serious part of the business seems to be the initial step. *Imprimis*, then, a man should place himself upon the most solid footing of respectability, establish a base of supplies, as it were, for cour-

age, advice, sympathy, and that calm dis-
criminating judgment which a woman pos-
sesses so pre-eminently more than a man—in
fact, a man should find an ally, or, in other
words, a wife." "To be sure," answered
Blaisdel, "that is, I suppose so, but it's so
confounded risky." "Risky?" interrogated
Hugh, over whose face an expression of
scorn shot for an instant. "Risky for whom,
pray—did you happen to mean for the woman,
Charlie? If you did, I say Amen." "Well,
that was not the idea that I had at the time
I spoke," retorted Blaisdel; "possibly she *was*
included in my estimate of risk, but I suppose I was thinking principally of myself,
you see, Hugh—" "Oh, yes, I see," interrupted Griswold, "that man is the most selfish
brute on earth in matters affecting his comfort, his convenience and his liberties—few
thoughts he ever gives to the woman in such
cases, except as to what he requires of her;
money, good looks, amiability, obedience to
his sovereign will, answering all questions,
asking none—risky! I should say it was, especially in these times, and for the woman, a

thousanu times more than for the man."
"Quixotic nonsense, all of that," replied
Blaisdel, emptying his glass of Cliquot, and
complaisantly regarding its replenishment;
"of course, marriage is a woman's natural
ambition, and if a man can offer her an honorable name, a comfortable home, good so-
ciety, what more can she desire?" "She can
desire a *great deal* more, Charlie, but she
rarely gets it. She can desire companionship
for one thing, and how much of that precious
commodity would the average city man of
to-day be willing to give, how many nights
would he be willing to dock from his club or
lodge to turn over to her, I should like to
ask; courtship stops too suddenly to my
thinking; the tenderness fades out of a man's
voice too often, when he supplants the word
. sweetheart with that of wife, and that's what
kills. To my notion, a woman's worth weighs
considerably over sixteen ounces to every
pound of that commodity which a man brings
into the market. Yes, marriage is risky,
risky for the woman." "My dear fellow,"
replied Blaisdel, a smile flitting across his

features, as he settled himself more comfortably in the arm-chair, and took a leisurely survey of the large, brilliantly lighted room, and of the pretty women it contained, " the championship of woman is an earnest of nobility, and heaven forbid that the name of Blaisdel should ever bear the taint of espousal of the cause of their oppressors, so often though

'The light that lies in woman's eyes
Has been my heart's undoing,'—

that it behoves me to approach with some deliberation and respect for the voice of warning, that period of a final decision, from which there is no retreat possible. Besides, a calm deliberation dignifies any act of a man's life, and what should be embellished with a greater dignity, than this all important one of marriage. A man wants to be sure of himself and her, before he asks a woman to take up the burden of life with him; he wants to be certain that this glamour which surrounds all things at such a time will last. Ik Marvel expresses it beautifully: ' Damp will deaden the fire of a cigar, and,

there are hellish damps, alas, too many, that
will deaden the early blazing of the heart.' "

"Charlie, you are a dreamer, and I believe
you will go on dreaming all your life, provided your dreams come to you tinged with
the light of sentimentality—but, life has more
than sentiment in its offering, and, one should
bar the door first, against want and hardship
and wrong, and sentiment will idle in on the
sunbeams through the window panes; but do
you know what time it is?   Eleven o'clock,
by all that's good, and that ball still before us."
"Plenty of time," said Blaisdel, "take some
more wine. No? So be it then, ours be the
intoxication which lies in a woman's smile,
and, if I mistake not, you will be very drunken
with it all before you leave the 'Academy,'
to-night, especially if Kitty is there, as I hope
she will be." "Kitty," said Hugh, "Kitty
who? That's rather an indefinite allusion
to a fair divinity." "Why, there's but *one*
Kitty in the world, man," said Blaisdel.
"Wait till you see Kitty Wilmerding, and, if
the list of the enslaved is not greater by one, all
my hope of you, Hugh, will perish on the spot."

Hugh Griswold had never taken any special pains to mask his feelings—his emotions, whether of joy or sorrow, had always quite naturally ranged themselves behind the bulwark of a quiet dignity of manner which was his by inheritance; rarely was he as outspoken as he had been to-night. People were generally with him free of their own views of life, and men had never failed in according him a similar prerogative. An impertinent curiosity was as foreign to his nature as a liberty toward himself would have been intolerable. Men liked him, and respected him in his quiet, undemonstrative ways, but no one dared to accept the risk of attempted familiarity; there was a light in his eyes which told of a spirit best left dormant. It is your quiet man who becomes dangerous when aroused. Hugh did not know that Kitty Wilmerding was in the city; he had thought of her as miles away—far off among the hills of New England, whither he would gladly have gone to her, to ask if the period of his probation had passed, but time was wanting; he had run on to New York only for a couple

of days to attend to some pressing business,
and must return at once, and, Charlie Blaisdel's announcement that she was in the city,
while it gave him infinite pleasure, came to
him in a way he did not exactly like. He did
not like to hear her name upon Charlie Blaisdel's flippant tongue, and it angered him.
"Miss Wilmerding in New York," he said, in
slow tones, looking straight into Blaisdel's
eyes. "I did not know that you knew her."
"Why, what's the matter, Hugh?" exclaimed
Blaisdel, "you look as though you had seen
a ghost. Of course, I know Kitty Wilmerding, and if I may judge from appearances, I
should say that her existence is neither a
matter of news or indifference to *you*." "In
both of which surmises you are correct," replied Hugh, and not willing to let Blaisdel
into the knowledge of his very great interest
in the young lady, he added, "and I congratulate you upon your own apparent intimacy
with her." "That's not the word, Hugh,"
said Blaisdel, "*that's* not the word by a long
shot. I don't think she has an *intimate* gentleman friend in the world, though there are

thousands who have striven hard enough for the honor. She doesn't seem to be in any hurry to relinquish her freedom, I can assure you. She is not the butterfly to be caught (yet at least), though many a man has thrown his net," and then, as though he was about to utter another thought he caught himself and indulged the mental reflection, "Can Hugh Griswold be the man who is holding her in check?"

CHAPTER II.

Who has ever set foot within that temple of
the muses, "The Academy of Music," without
a feeling of awe, as though in the presence of
the masters whose inspirations, through the
interpretations of the most God-gifted artists
of the earth, have called forth the plaudits of
wondering millions! It is as though one trod
upon hallowed ground, and, lingering upon
the air, dulcet memories of such voices as
those of Grisi, and Mario and Jenny Lind, and
La Grange, Parepa, Tamberlik and Brignoli
whisper of a triumphant past. As Griswold,
late in the evening, stepped into the auditor-
ium the scene that met his eye was one of ex-
ceeding beauty. All that art could accomplish, with flowers and costly draperies, with
paintings and priceless soul-pictures, with
bunting and burnished arms, with tapestries
and silken hangings, with light and softened
radiance, was there to charm the sense and
soul. In the boxes, ranged tier upon tier,

women looked down upon the scene in animated conversation, the melody of many a silvery voice falling in grateful accents upon the ear. Here was the flash of countless jewels, the rhythmic motion of a thousand fans, the power and influence of music ; the subtle incense which pervades the realm of woman. Amidst all these, happiness in her speaking eyes, the glory of her lovely womanhood enwrapping her as in a mantle, sat she, whom in all the earth he loved the best. She was speaking, as he looked, to Blaisdel, and evidently his latest remark had come to her in the light of a surprise, not a disagreeable one, either, if Hugh interpreted her looks aright, but whether *he* was the subject of the conversation, of course he could not tell. He stood and looked at her for a few moments. There was a pleasure to him in even this distant view of the woman he loved. It pleased him to see the look of happiness upon her face—the light of an innocent soul looking from out her large, blue eyes—the every graceful movement of her body, rhythmic like a willow in the swaying of a gentle breeze.

Evidently Blaisdel's talk was pleasing to her, as it was to most women, when he had the will to make it so, and Hugh felt a pang as near akin to jealousy as he had ever felt, while he looked.

A few moments later he knocked at the door of the box and entered, and was repaid instanter, for Kitty had risen and given him her hand in welcome.

"Oh, Mr. Griswold, what a charming surprise. I could scarcely credit Mr. Blaisdel when he told me you would be here; I had thought of you as far away somewhere in a horrid tent, undergoing no end of hardships." "Thank you for the assurance that you have thought of me at all, Miss Wilmerding," said Hugh; "my tent would contain no discomforts could I know that you followed me sometimes there in your thoughts." "Why, of course, what more can we women do, than think of our absent heroes," she answered; "I hope you have come to stay some time, now that you are here." "Until to-morrow," Hugh replied; "but in the pleasure of seeing *you* there is more than compensation for the

shortness of my stay." Blaisdel had turned
and engaged one of the other ladies in conversation, so that he did not hear when
Kitty remarked: "Don't pay compliments,
do not deteriorate from the style of man I
knew a year ago. One is surfeited with compliments here." "Need there have been an
idle compliment in my words?" said Hugh.
"A year ago I told you what you were to me,
and I have not changed—is there any need
that I should, Kitty?—have I no right to
think of you as I did?" "You have every
right to think of me as kindly as you will,"
she said, "and there is no likelihood of
there being any one to dispute that right."
And with this much Hugh was constrained
to be satisfied, for half a dozen people
crowded into the box at this moment, and
the conversation became general nor did he
have an opportunity of an uninterrupted
talk that night, only in bidding her good-
bye some time later, he had looked down
into her eyes and said: "Good-bye, I am
happier after having seen you again. You
will follow me sometimes in your thoughts,

will you not, and I may still have hope to comfort me?" "I shall think of you often—pray for you—always—pray that the future may have no disappointments in store for you —or for me," she answered and her little hand rested for an instant, passively within his own, and as her eyes looked up at him, as through a mist, his heart spoke to her through the mysterious agency of a gentle pressure, and he was gone.

———

Moored to the long rickety wharf at Belle Plains, upon the Potomac River, one of a flotilla of craft of similar construction, the canal-boat "& Ru Jaxn" awaited a cargo. There was an easy grace and majestic bearing withal about this craft, different from the forbidding lack of compromise in the black hulls and straight lines of her sisters; she sat upon the placid waters imbued with some suggestions of a thing of life, her bows up-reared, breasting the stream as though impatient of testing her strength against some cresting wave, her sheer line, long and graceful, and her projecting stern overhanging the untroubled waters, the material sequence of some happy understanding between the ship-wright and his workmen. Proud she was, too, in the matter of personal adornment, a broad, white stripe relieving the darkness of her hull, and, in golden letters, she carried upon her stern-post the emblazonry of her historic name. What mattered it if that name disclosed, in its orthography, departure from the tenets of an established school: was not the name itself sufficient warrant of a bold refusal of servile imitation and adherence to anterior custom? With prescriptive right she looked with scorn upon the feeble efforts of such names as " Dolly" and " Alice Jane " and "Phoebe S." and others of the ilk; in es-tablishing a personality, *she* boasted of a name which had been proudly upon the lips of every born American, and high in the air she flaunted it in the face of all beholders. Her captain, a staunch old New England sailor, had long since deserted the stormy seas, and settled quietly aboard the "& Ru Jaxn," content with his good-tempered, worthy wife, to pass his remaining days amidst scenes of a less

exciting nature. Captain Jenkins was a man
too wise in his generation, and with a fund
of anecdote and personal adventure, which
he was fond of sharing with an attentive audience, under the mollifying influences of a pipe
and occasional glass of grog. And now the
"& Ru Jaxn" had left the narrow boundaries
of her accustomed routes, and her owner,
won over by prospective gain, had yielded to
the requirements of a pressing governmental
need, and swung her into line in readiness
for a new and hazardous enterprise.

There was a motley assemblage of craft at
Belle Plains; ferry-boats, and steam-barges,
tugs and canal-boats awaited the coming of
two divisions of the Ninth Army Corps,
which, by special request of their old commander, General Burnside, were being trans-
ferred from the Army of the Potomac to the
West. They were to embark at Belle Plains,
rendezvous and equip at Newport News at
the mouth of the James River, and thence
proceed to Baltimore, *en route* to their destination. Late one evening of early Spring, long
lines of infantry filed along down the winding,

corduroy road to the river bank; batteries of artillery and wagon trains went into park wherever the nature of the ground admitted, and as rapidly as possible the work of embarkation was accomplished. The "& Ru Jaxn" and three sometime liners on the canal, fitted for the reception of horses, were loaded with the animals of two batteries, and as the tug steamed out into the stream with its odd tow, three rousing cheers from the soldiers bivouacked upon the decks bade farewell to that grand army, which escaped from the jaws of death, lay resting from their heroic but ineffectual attempts at Fredericksburg. To Captain Griswold had been assigned this singular section of an odd flotilla; his battery horses had been loaded, and he and his lieutenant, Clarence Olmstead, were to be passengers on the "& Ru Jaxn," and she, bringing up the rear of the procession, would give them supervision of the whole. Griswold rather looked forward with pleasure to the trip; there would be the charm of novelty about it, and dullness, with Olmstead aboard, would be impossible, for he was a wild, fun-

loving fellow with a fertility of resource in
that direction never found wanting. He, too,
was genuinely fond of Griswold and had
studied him sufficiently to know when "Old
Hugh," as he styled him, wanted to be left to
his own thoughts, and so the two got on
splendidly together. But Hugh's anticipation of a quiet time, a time for thought, and
the maturing of some half-formed plans for
the future, were destined to disappointment.

He had gone below into the little cabin,
over which Mrs. Jenkins, as tutelar deity of
the craft presided, and had received from
that worthy dame the assignment of his berth
which he was making comfortable after his
own fashion, with the assistance of his fac-
totum, a small, red-headed Irishman who, as
a *striker*, had no superior, and few equals.
"It's luxury you'll be havin' here, Capten,"
remarked the irrepressible son of Erin, "faith
it's loike Noah's Ark, barrin' the absence of
some of the animals." "Hush, Flynn," said
Griswold, "I am talking to Mrs. Jenkins." "I
beg pardin, sor, no disrespect to yourself or
the lady; the ark was surely a foine place

and Mistress Noah a foine woman, though
I'm told her temper was tried at toimes."
With which complimentary remark and
characteristic satisfaction at having the last
word, Flynn disappeared up the companion-
way to the deck.

"I hope we are not incommoding you, Mrs.
Jenkins," said Griswold.

"Oh, no, sir; not in the least. I'm used to
having the cabin crowded; she has berths for
a dozen, you see, and often we have carried
more—me and Israel likes company."

"Naturally enough," remarked Hugh, "it
must be dull work upon the canal, I should
say."

"It is home to me *now*," answered the good
woman. "I could not bear to stay alone at
the old place, and Israel had to have work.
We buried our only child, a girl of fourteen,
three years ago, and the house was never the
same to either of us after that. It's only them
as has lost their children knows how dear
they was," and a flood of tender memories,
a sudden home-coming of her sense of sad
bereavement dimmed the old lady's eyes, and

as she removed her spectacles and wiped them, she said :

"You have no family, sir ? "

"No—none, Mrs. Jenkins, some day, per-haps, I may be so far blessed," said Hugh.

"Aye, I see, sir, you have your heart on some nice girl, no doubt; she must be worry-ing for you these sad times."

"It would make me very happy to think so, Mrs. Jenkins. What the d——!" which abrupt termination to Hugh's outspoken thought and his exclamation of surprise was due to the unceremonious manner of Lieu-tenant Clarence Olmstead's entrance, or rather descent, into the cabin.

"Hoop-la ! " shouted that impetuous young man, as he sprang down the steps, touching them but once in his flight; "beg pardon, Mrs. Jenkins; yours, too, Captain, but we're in *such* luck."

"Out with it, then," exclaimed Hugh, "but please remember that I am in a way respon-sible for your neck, which you seem to care very little for, judging from the manner of your descent of those steps; now what is it?"

"Why the steamer with the guns has just gone, and an old gentleman with his two daughters, who had hoped to go to Fortress Monroe aboard of her, are left, and Captain Jenkins has just agreed to take them down with us, if you're agreeable, and you will be of course—they seem to be such nice people. He has something to do with the Christian Commission, I believe, and is traveling with his daughters through the army, and one of them is fair as Aurora, sweet as Dorothy Dean; the other, dark as Nourmahal and handsome as Psyche."

"Strange place for ladies, it seems to me," replied Hugh, "but that is their affair; of course, I have no objection if they think they can stand it. Go on deck and entertain them Olmstead, while Mrs. Jenkins and I consult as to ways and means," and, turning to that somewhat astonished matron, Hugh explained that his mess chest was well supplied, and that Flynn was a capital cook, so no doubt they should get along. Shortly after, Hugh went on deck, and there met the kindly old gentleman, his face fairly beaming

with benevolence, and his daughters—they
were, indeed, exceedingly handsome women,
the elder, probably twenty-five years of age,
tall, graceful, and with a quiet dignity of
manner in marked contrast with the buoyant
spirits of her sister, whom Olmstead had
monopolized quite as a matter of course, and
who seemed to look upon their prospective
voyage as no end of fun.

The descent of the river was not to be begun till morning. The oddly freighted tow
had pulled out into the stream and swung
around in the current and come to anchor,
and only waited the morning light to steam
away toward its destination. The nights
were chilly yet, and the party early adjourn-
ed to the cabin and seated around on lockers
and valises, devoted themselves to becoming
better acquainted. Olmstead contrived to
get his divinity off in one corner and, dis-
dainful of methods of regular approach, pro-
ceeded to storm the citadel of that young lady's heart after his own characteristic fashion.
To Griswold, the old gentleman was a fascin-
ation—the story of his connection with the

Christian Commission; the scenes of tragedy
and pathos to which he had been witness in
camp and hospital; the labors of his col-
leagues in the field of benevolence and amel-
ioration of the sufferings of sick and wounded
possessed for him a thrilling interest, and
when he referred with pardonable pride to
his elder daughter's patient watchfulness and
tender nursing within the wards of the
Washington hospitals, there rose up before
Hugh's mind the sweet womanliness of that
inspiration of Owen Meredith's La Sœur
Seraphine, reproduced in the lovely woman
at his side, whose dark beauty shed a radiance about her:

" Like the light upon Autumn's soft shadowy days."

But everybody was tired out and glad to
go to rest after the wearying day, and Hugh
and Olmstead soon found themselves pacing
the deck in the enjoyment of a pipe, while
the ladies took advantage of their absence to
creep into their berths, and give themselves
up to the " god of dreams."

A gentle breeze swept over the surface of

the water, throwing the tiny reflections of
the stars into the mazes of a merry dance,
while, from the blazing camp fires along the
shore bright gleams shot out upon the tide,
gilding the sides of the transports as they
swung gently at anchor in the moving
stream. There were but few tents visible.
Rolled in their blankets, the weary troops
lay down with no other covering but the
canopy of heaven—the soft murmur of the
wind, the musical lapping of the moving tide,
their lullaby.

CHAPTER III.

From the cabin of the "& Ru Jaxn" a door led forward into the kitchen, the special province of good Mrs. Jenkins, and here, before that worthy woman had opened her eyes, Flynn had established himself among the pots and pans with which he kept up a running fire of conversation, as though suddenly brought into friendly contact with friends of a by-gone day.

Nor was Flynn the only early riser aboard this stately craft. Lieutenant Clarence Olmstead had impressed upon the mind of Miss Marjorie Hale some idea of the extreme beauty of sunrise upon the Potomac, a picture to which his rich gift of imagination lent a coloring, pardonable possibly, in view of the result which he hoped for, of stimulating that young lady's appetite for breakfast by the copious drafts of fresh morning air, which a turn or two of the deck would insure, and so he had said *"Good night"* the

evening before, only to bemoan the fact, that
several hours must elapse before he could
say *"Good morning,"* and in anticipation of
this matutinal greeting, he was now pacing
the deck, humming a little French song,
which had suggested itself to his impatient
thoughts as appropriate to the occasion:

"Le rideau de ma voisine;
Se souleve lentement,
Elle va, je L'imagine,
Prendre l'air un moment."

And this musical reminder of her promise
coming to the awakening sense of the young
lady, she slipped quietly from her berth and
very soon stood before him, as sweet and
fresh as an early blossom of May. "Oh,
Miss Marjorie, good morning," said Olmstead, "I hope you have slept well. The sun
has been impatient of your coming and
rushes to embrace you." "He is quite im-
partial in his favors though," answered his
companion, "but I am grateful for those he
lavishes on me. Oh! how lovely this is, I
must call my sister to enjoy it, too." "Really, I would not, Miss Marjorie, I am sure she

needs rest. She appeared quite fagged out last night, and besides, gratify my selfishness and carry the remembrance of *this* morning as of one whose beauties I invoked for *you*."

" And are your invocations always so happy of result, Mr. Olmstead?" and pretty Marjorie Hale laughed as musically as a song bird in its greeting to the day.

"Content yourself with this one exhibition of my powers, please. One should never tempt the gods too far," said Olmstead. And indeed, the sight was beautiful, and Marjorie Hale drank it all in with a pure girlish delight. The long stretch of water before them shimmered in the sunlight like a surface of frosted gold; the tall spars of sloops and schooners, as they rode at anchor, cast their shadows far astern. The decks were peopled with busy throngs of men; along the shore and deep within the density of the woods, the troops were responding to the bugle notes which roused them into activity; on the air were the faint odors of the morning meal, steaming above a hundred camp-fires; voices in morning salutation and snatches of song

routed the stillness which had boded over
the scene. Far down the river in a graceful
curve the waters passed from view, leaving
upon the horizon but a stretch of forest
trees, their gilded tops nodding in the moving winds in clear reflection against the distant, cloudless sky.

A moment later, Flynn, the irrepressible,
well-schooled as to human needs, and with
full measure of that national characteristic
which esteems the service of a woman para-
mount to all other obligations, appeared coming up the companion-way with a steaming
hot cup of coffee, which he offered to Miss
Marjorie, remarking: " You'd better thry this,
Miss; it's a panacaer against the ills of the
morning air; its tay the lieutenent takes,
and he's had his dra—cup, I mean, already,"
and with a twinkle in his eye, as he looks at
Olmstead, he drops down again amidst the
pots and pans. But Marjorie is none the
wiser of Olmstead's matutinal tipple, which
Flynn had so nearly disclosed, and she only
laughs and says: " What a droll fellow
your servant is, Mr. Olmstead; he must be

an unending source of entertainment to you, but it was very kind of him to bring me this delicious coffee."

" Yes," replied Olmstead, " he is a typical Irishman, and never at a loss for a word, though he handles his vocabulary with surprising recklessness at times. You will find him quite your devoted slave, Miss Marjorie, as we will all be, if you will permit. You have but to command to be obeyed."

"How very nice you are, indeed," answered the young girl, as she sipped her coffee, and, looking far over the water in the wake of their singular procession (for they were moving now down stream), added : " Oh, how happy I am ; how beautiful all this seems ! "

And Olmstead, watching her as she sat there, the delicate glow of perfect health upon her cheeks, the light of a happy content in her speaking eyes, one dainty little hand lying upon the rail of the vessel, a pretty little foot peeping from beneath her gown, and seemingly keeping time to the rhythmic cadence of her thoughts, made a mental resolve, touching upon a very important factor, in the shaping of his future life.

Meanwhile, Captain Jenkins had been busied with matters connected with his tow; looking to the adjustments of the ropes, the stowing on deck of the fenders, the securing of the hatches so as to admit light and air to the animals, and had, finally, ensconced himself upon a stool beside the tiller, and, here, with his pipe in active operation, he presented a picture of perfect content, and, chiming in with Marjorie's expression of delight at the peaceful beauty of the scene outspread before them, emitted dense clouds of smoke by way of preparation and preface to his remark.

"It's pretty, Miss, enough, but it lacks the life—it lacks the life." "Why, Captain Jenkins, how can you say that, it seems full of life to me, and of beauty too; but I suppose you miss the sea with all its dangers and excitements," said Marjorie, as she looked back at him and adjusted a refractory curl which had escaped from beneath her broad Gainsborough hat.

"Yes, yes, Miss, that's it, I suppose. It's

often dull aboard a craft like this, and we don't often have a blythe young lass to cheer us up," and the old sailor puffed vigorously at his pipe, as though to reward himself for having said just the right thing. "Now, Captain Jenkins, if you are going to turn flatterer, too," and she flashed with her bright blue eyes a warning signal at Olmstead, who was rather impatient of this disturbance of his tête-a-tête, " I shall think I have not a *true* friend on board."

"Little doubt of that, Miss ; there's the lieutenant there, looks as though he'd champion ye and bless the chance," and with a quiet little chuckle this observant man of the sea lashed the tiller and moved away to the forward part of the boat where something seemed to need his attention.

" Mr. Olmstead," said Marjorie, "do men *ever* grow too old for flattery ?" " Never, that I heard of," laughed Olmstead, "they recognize the fact, that it is an essential feature to some women's happiness ; but I can scarcely conceive of your being subject to its annoyance ; what would be subtle flattery to

many another woman would be but simple
truth to you."

"What wondrous powers of analysis you
have, Mr. Olmstead; here, you have known
me for about twelve hours, and you have
assigned me an established character already:
thank you, sir; but, I fear you will find me
very commonplace and human before our
voyage ends," laughed the young lady, who
secretly hoped she was not doomed to disappointment in the handsome fellow before
her, for Marjorie Hale hated flattery above
all things, as it had to her the ring of insin-
cerity which she could not tolerate in any
human being; her very soul spoke out
through her great blue eyes, and she was
provokingly pretty and attractive, but she
was a remarkably well-balanced young lady
withal, and knew the sound of true metal
when she heard it; but, happily, Olmstead's
threatened confession was averted by the
appearance of the rest of the party on deck,
and a few moments later, Flynn's announcement of breakfast.

There was one thing, which Olmstead never

parted from, and that was his guitar. Fortun-
ately, the facilities for transporting it were
ample in his battery, and many a weary in-
fantryman, as he trudged along with the
assignment of the twentieth part of a mule as
transportation for such of his belongings as
were upon his person, has looked with pardonable envy upon the good-sized wagon
rolling by with every battery, disclosing
evidences of prospective comfort, nay, luxury,
when camp should be reached. Within this
wagon Olmstead had always carefully stowed
his guitar-box, and many a night his skillful
handling of it, and the accompaniment of his
fine mellow, tenor voice, had made those
within the compass of its tones forget their
weariness and drop off to a sweet, restful
sleep, peopled with the voices and faces of
loved ones far away.

Hugh, too, would possibly have been guilty
of the surreptitious expenditure of certain
stores not absolutely essential, rather than
have left Olmstead's guitar behind, consider-
ing it, as he had often told fhat hair-brained
youth, "his most material claim to rational

ity," and often, when he was weary and worried, and the world seemed out of tune, he had dropped down on Olmstead's bed with the simple remark, " Play something, youngster," and would close his eyes and listen, and go out after awhile, comforted. There was nothing of the romantic in Hugh Griswold's nature; but there was, underlying his quiet, undemonstrative way, a depth of feeling which few people ever suspected; his sensibilities were singularly acute; life and its duties and its pleasures he looked upon as obligations; but, not as obligations to be fulfilled in a scornful or careless manner. To him there was beneath the outer covering of most things something beyond sight or touch; beauties, whether of soul or sense, which it was the duty of life to discover, not only to one's self, but to others; harmonies to be evolved out of the seeming discords and entanglements of life's perplexities. Hugh never seemed conscious of the unsightly evidences of ignorance or poverty; his eye looked back beyond effect to cause; to the pathetic, not the repulsive manifestations of what he esteemed a human wrong. He was no idle dreamer, however—no visionary. It was a manly hand with which he grasped the implements for his life's work; nothing could swerve him when duty called, and, through example, he could honestly exact a following. Stern, he had been known to be, but with no one more than with himself; yet, in many things, he had the delicate instincts and manner of a woman. Upon the battlefield, men looked to him as to a pillar of strength, and never found him wanting; and, in the hospitals, his coming had brightened many an eye, and, under his gentle ministrations, men past help had given him a grateful look—they could not speak—and closed their eyes with resignation when their friend was near.

Breakfast over, everybody acknowledged the superior attractions of the deck, except good Mrs. Jenkins, and she and Flynn having established a very friendly understanding over the preparations for the *morning* meal, organized themselves into a committee of ways and means for the further relief for that particular portion of hungry humanity, within the limited sphere of their little world. The others paired off according to natural affinity and Marjorie and Olmstead strolled about in an absent sort of way till the others should have comfortably settled themselves, having an eye to their own subsequent establishment upon the basis of most probable non-interruption. Captain Jenkins, having secured an audience, albeit of one, fairly beamed over the prospect of the exercise of his conversational powers. Madelaine Hale and Hugh, far aft, were comfortably ensconced upon the acceptable substitute for a steamer rug which a Navajo blanket afforded and Marjorie and Olmstead, having returned from an inspection of the state of the *men's* bivouac and a peep down the hatches at the surprised and indignant horses, dropped down, a short time later on, beside the roof over the companion-way. Madelaine Hale was something of an artist, and Hugh had managed to rig up a little awning for her, under which she was sketching the distant river banks, the broad, beautiful stream and this odd flotilla upon its bosom, to be reserved

as a convincing proof to any unbeliever to
whom she might at some future day disclose
the history of this singular voyage. Hugh
watched her as she worked, watched her
sweet, sad face, the deft handling of her
pencil, the play of her mobile features upon
which the lights and shadows as they fell
told something of her thoughts and he wondered what sorrow had come to her:

"Had the pansies withered she used to know;
And the roses faded—of long ago,"

and he thought of Balzac's comparison between ripe womanhood and Indian summer,
and, applying it to her, seemed to see how the
beautiful buds of promise and of hope, bereft
of summer's opening breath, had caught
within their enfoldings, the tints which are the
heralds of decay. Intent upon her work, she
was not conscious of Hugh's scrutiny. She
appeared enamored of the task before her,
only at times in the intervals of the completion of one and the commencement of a second feature of her sketch, she would lift her
eyes for an instant and seem to be looking far

away over the water; far beyond the blue outline of the distant hills into a land, a creation
of her own, whither none might follow her,
and, then, with a smile at Hugh, would address him some simple remark and fall to
sketching once more.

But Hugh was content, the quiet chimed
in very acceptably with his mood, and loung-
ing here upon the deck, the soft warm breeze
speaking of quick advancing Spring and
bringing into grateful life all things upon
which had lain the blight of wintry weather;
within the compass of that atmosphere which,
in a distinct but subtle way, marks a lovely
woman's presence; with a momentary sense
of relief from care or the necessity of action,
his own thoughts back to where he had last
seen, in all her girlish charm, the woman
within whose hand lay the power of shaping
the course of his future journeyings, he was
happy as any *present* surroundings could have
made him. But he and his companion are
suddenly recalled from their wanderings, the
pencil falls from the dainty hand, Hugh re-
moves his pipe from between his lips sending

a cloud of smoke curling away over the stern of the vessel and both of them listen. For upon the air in perfect harmony, two young voices, low and sweet, with that accompaniment which speaks of southern suns and flowers and love, break upon the silence in sweet and sad refrain:

> " Falling leaf and fading tree,
> Lines of white in a sullen sea,
> Shadows rising on you and me,
> Shadows rising on you and me,"

and as she listens, Madelaine Hale has that far away look again, and her cheek is ashen pale and her hands are pressed upon her bosom, and far across the water the sad words :

> " What are we waiting for, you and I,
> A pleading look, a stifled cry.
> Good-bye, forever ; good-bye, forever,
> Good-bye;"

fade away in the distance ; the song is over, and she, unable to bear the strain, buries her face in her hands and weeps aloud.

CHAPTER IV.

Hugh Griswold is appalled. There was a dimness of outline in the things he himself looked upon due to the suspicion of moisture within his own eyes, for the song brought back to him, as though it had been yesterday, a farewell which he had spoken, but not forever; oh, no. Fate had nothing so cruel in store for him. But Madelaine! To *her* the words brought back a flood of sad, tender memories, all that was left her now. He saw it all. Death had robbed that trusting, faithful heart of all that was most dear to it. Poor girl—poor girl, he thought, I see now the cause of all her sadness. What should he do? He could resist a charge; could stand up against the brunt of battle, but a woman in tears unnerved him, unmanned him.

"Miss Hale," he said, "for heaven's sake do not cry, I'm so sorry for you; will you not be comforted. Surely this world has yet much in store for you."

" I beg your pardon, Captain Griswold. I have no right to bring my troubles to others," sobbed the fair girl. " It only comes back to me so cruelly. Go away, please, for a little while and do not let *them* know," pointing to Marjorie and Olmstead, who, all unconscious of the mischief they had done, were evidently preparing for another burst of melody.

Hugh got up and sauntered to where the men were seated about in groups, playing cards, smoking and telling stories. He inspected the messes, looked in at the horsse, and then stood gazing out over the water and watched a flock of ducks fly by, swift and straight from some feeding ground ; listened to the soft plash of the water upon the bows; to the labored puffing of their tug drawing them along through the smooth waters, away from their winter's cheerless camps upon the Rappahannock; away from comrades in that grand army, which undaunted in the face of hardship and disaster proudly unfurled its standards, confident that upon their eagles would fall the ulti-

mate crown of victory. They steamed on
past the long wooded stretches of the bluffs
and low lying marsh—lands and bordering
densities of primeval forest where are:

> " The murmuring pines and the hemlock,
> Bearded with moss and in garments green,"

rounded a bold promontory upreared in
jealous guardianship of the tryst which the
river, further on, is keeping with the sea;
now following the wavering caprices of the
stream as it idles in the shadows of the land,
or darts away into the golden sunshine to
greet the breezes, which

> " have been out upon the deep at play."

Lost in his own thoughts, Hugh stood
some time oblivious to his surroundings till,
at last, casting his eyes toward where Madelaine sat, he saw her at her work again, and,
in a moment more, had dropped down beside her.

" Shall you probably be long at Fortress
Munroe, Miss Hale? ' he asked.

" Hardly, I think," she answered. " Papa
can scarcely spare much time from home.
He brought us away principally that I might
recruit my health, which has suffered some

from the confinement of the hospitals."

"But you will not return to them, surely," Hugh said, "it is a lovely sacrifice certainly for a woman to make, a beautiful devotion to a cause which appeals to all the noblest and gentlest impulses of her nature—but you owe a duty to yourself and to those to whom you are near and dear. However sweet the guerdon be, following the bestowal of her tender offices, a woman, adopting the role of nurse, should be very certain that she has not higher duties in another sphere, and, pardon me, I believe you have."

"I am happiest in the wards of the hospitals, Captain Griswold. I may be able to do more for others than could be done for me," she answered; "this war has brought to me the legacy of sorrow and bereavement. If I can spare another, through care and nursing, the misery which its lack has sent to me, life will not seem all in vain."

"You are a noble woman," Hugh answered, "happiness *will* come back to you some day. It is, I know, waiting now at the door for you to open."

Madelaine had laid aside her sketch and taken up a book, a little volume of poems, and began to idly turn over the leaves. The wind was freshening. Tiny flecks of foam, here and there, like daisies in the meadow grasses, accented the green coloring of the waters; the clouds were banking in the western sky; on the shores, the tree-tops nodded, and the forest voices were astir upon the air. Madelaine said she would go down for a shawl, and passing by where Marjorie and Olmstead sat, discovered the former, well protected in the latter's *army cape*, while the latter was giving her an insight into things military, which she seemed very much to enjoy. "Why, Madelaine! have you and Captain Griswold been discussing state secrets. You have been so quiet, we have been obliged to almost whisper, ourselves, for fear of disturbing you."

"Nothing very serious, Margie," replied her sister. "Captain Griswold has been giving me some very interesting thoughts of his to ponder over. I am going now for a shawl, it is getting cold."

"Yes," said Marjorie, "and Captain Jenkins has been looking all about like a weather prophet, and says he thinks there will
be rough weather on the bay. Think of a
canal boat in a storm." And here Captain
Jenkins himself came by and, hearing the
last part of this remark, said: "Oh, never
fear, we will not venture into rough water;
we'll go to anchor somewhere till the blow
is over," which quite comforted the ladies
who had no relish for anything more agi-
tating than the long heaving swells which
already were making themselves apparent.
Hugh concluded to leave Madelaine to her
book and to write some letters. He knew
he should be busied with a thousand things
when they reached Newport News, and
might not find time and, besides, here, he
could have all the quiet he desired, or that
was necessary for the framing of *one* letter
upon which he had been thinking a good
deal of late. It was a letter to Kitty Wilmerding. He loved her and she knew it.
She had told him that there was none to
question his right to think of her as he did,

and yet she had given him no promise that she would ever be other than a friend to him. He had respected her appeal to him to wait, for more than a year now, and he could stand it no longer. If there was any blow to his hopes in store for him it had better fall now than later on, when perhaps his strength to bear it would be weakened by the daily increasing passion that he felt for her. So he would write and ask her, in so many words, what he had asked her once before and she had failed to answer.

"Dear Kitty :" he wrote, " This letter will come to you in the light of a continuance of an interview, short and unsatisfactory, which chance afforded me when, a few days since, I was in New York. Had I known of your presence there before the very night of the ball at the 'Academy of Music,' I should have sought a meeting unembarrassed by those surroundings which assured a constant interruption, for I had much to say to you. When I left you, over a year ago, taking with me what comfort I could glean from your answer to my asking that you would be my wife, it seemed to me as though, for both our sakes, waiting were the better course, and I did try faithfully to carry out your wishes in the matter. But many months have passed since then and waiting is weary work, especially when one has only the distractions of danger and of hardship to tide over the waiting days. You are surrounded by friends, pleasurable excitements and admirers, and I rejoice that it is so. I begrudge you none of them. I love to think of you as happy and hedged about by fostering care and that on your pathway fall sweet blossoms as you pass. I love to think of you as I saw you last upon the hills overlooking that pretty New England village where I met you first, the autumn tints about you, a rich, dark setting to the gentler suggestion of the perfect May. But cannot you conceive of my longing for something *more* than a tender thought of you; my longing for possession and the promise that will insure it to me later on? I will not press you farther. You know full well that every ambition of my life centres in the hope that when the war is over you will be the gentle companion of my life. Kitty, you have given me hope, give me more. Tell me that my patient waiting has not been in vain; let me feel that life has in store for me something beyond the day's allotted task. I am writing upon the deck of a canal boat, one of four which are being towed to Newport News with the battery horses. With us is a Mr. Hale, a member of the Christian Commission and, will you believe it, his two daughters, lovely girls, and Olmstead, of whom I have so often spoken to you, if *not* in the toils, simulates it to perfection.

We had hoped to reach our destination to-morrow, but there is every indication now of an enforced delay, as the wind is rising and the Chesapeake will most probably be in too great a state of commotion for a canal boat to venture out with safety, so we shall probably lie by and here will come the difficult problem of getting water to the horses, so even life on a canal boat is not at all times one of indolence and ease. I shall look for your reply before we start West, and Oh!

Kitty, let it be such as will accord to me the right to come back to you when I may, in nearer and dearer relationship than as

Your friend,

HUGH GRISWOLD."

When he had finished his writing, Hugh put the letter in his pocket, ready for dropping into the mail when the voyage came to an end and, having accomplished that which had occupied his thoughts for many days, he lit his pipe and settled himself upon deck in an easier, more contented frame of mind than he had known since the night when, with music and light and incense upon the air, he had turned his back upon the bewildering fascinations of the great city.

Very shortly after, Flynn again came upon the scene with the welcome announcement of dinner. The bracing air had sharpened the appetites of the travelers, and they were prepared to give evidence of their appreciation to whatsoever was set before them. Flynn, upon this occasion, too, displayed accomplishments which had evidently been held in reserve for some special oppor-

tunity of expression, like the present. His
hair, which had hitherto been innocent of the
faintest suggestion of part, now fell away at
either side of a conspicuous line of separation, which acted so strongly in the nature
of a disguise as nearly to conceal his identity.
With the assistance of Mrs. Jenkins, he was
resplendent in a white apron of curious and
original design, while a red silk handkerchief,
which encircled his neck, lent its own rich
hue toward the establishment of a unique
and striking personality. But Flynn's metal
was up, and he was determined that "The
Captain" should have a glimpse of the possibilities centering in his person, not only in
matters pertaining to dress, but in the cuis-
ine, and some of the dishes he presented
were models of flavor and combination, and
the ornamental embellishments of a fowl with
white and red vegetable roses, which he
skilfully carved, proclaimed him an artist of
no mean pretensions. The dinner passed off
very pleasantly and with much merriment on
the part of Marjorie and Olmstead, notwith-
standing the solemnity with which the magni-

ficence of Flynn was supposed to invest it, but Marjorie could no more refrain from laughing than a bird can from singing, and the funny things of life never escaped her.

Flynn, indeed, was a typical striker, a man equal to any emergency. The active partner in the concern of which Griswold was the head. The Army striker is a man but little known to the outside world; he is as different from ordinary humanity as man is different from his Darwinian prototype. Nationality has nothing to do with the composition of a striker. He is "sui generis," one of nature's happy thoughts or inspirations, an indispensable requisite, to every well-regulated military household. There is something about his gait, a certain expression of the eye, betokening calm under all conditions, and a disdain of mess-room frivolties which marks the man, as the predestined ruler of your household, second, indeed, in command to your wife (if you have one), who, by virtue of inherent right and natural tendency, is *first*, in the order of government. This man is the moving spirit of the

establishment, so far as its routine goes. He
attends to your lamps, sees that the supply
of oil and fuel is kept up ; milks your cow
and consults with your cook as to items
needed from the Commissary ; sees that the
prisoners perform their allotted tasks of split-
ting your wood, emptying your refuse barrels, and policeing your yards and keeps an
eye meanwhile on your chicken house, to
guard against their yielding to temptation.
This is the being whom you can hear from
your dining-room, as the meal progresses
(especially if you have company), talking
low to your cook, giving practical evidence
of his approval of her talents as the various
courses are brought out, and who, between
mouthful and remark, nicks a plate in true
soldier fashion. He is the ever patient being who stands ready to receive unlimited
invective, when prudence suggests the in-
appropriateness of an in-door explosion. He
guards your household and your children, if
you are absent, awaiting your return oblivious of the hour, and if you are a bachelor,
often unites in his own person, the qualities of

valet and of chef. He is a long suffering, patient, ever active being, without either nerves or knowledge of fatigue, who guards your interests with watch-dog fidelity, and for whom, from the nature of things, you have a very warm place in your heart.

To Marjorie, Flynn had appeared "no end of fun," but in the light of all that Olmstead told her, of his fidelity and the various functions he assumed, she came to regard him as a veritable prodigy; a man to be looked up to, as possessing qualities of a superior order.

"Only think, Mr. Olmstead, if he were killed, what would you do?" she asked.

"Take an inventory of my effects and begin life over again," replied Olmstead. "Indeed, it's a calamity I do not like to contemplate." But there was no lingering at table, the swells from the bay were sensibly affecting the stability of their craft, and the close air of the cabin was undesirable, so the ladies concluded to have their coffee on deck, and thither the whole party repaired. Before them and around them the white caps,

"Like the wings of sea birds"

dotted the surface of the water. The cloud bank in the west had broken into disordered masses, which scudded before the rising winds; the river was widening in its near approach to the bay; far distant, a towering light-house stood out against the sky; the river bluffs had dropped behind, and low wooded stretches confine the waters at either hand. In the bay beyond, huge waves were tumbling together in wild disorder, a vessel in the offing, storm tossed, was making for anchorage within the capes; in the hold, the horses were giving signs of distress and impatience, but the discomfiture was short-lived, and a couple of hours before dark they were drawn into the smooth waters of the St. Mary's river and had come to anchor. It was Saturday afternoon, and the Captain informed Griswold that even in the event of the wind's subsidence it would not be safe to venture out into the Chesapeake before Monday, so they had a prospective delay of thirty-six hours at least. It was well enough so far as the passengers were concerned; they were in no particular hurry; time was passing pleasantly enough for them, and Olmstead, in fact, had told Marjorie not long before, that he wished it might last for ever, but the poor horses who had no water since starting were doubtless contrary-minded, and Hugh's *first* thought was of them. The St. Mary's river was hardly more than a good-sized stream, widening at the mouth to something like a hundred yards, forming a snug harbor for the small flotilla, sheltering it from the wind and waves, a "perfect Sunday harbor," Marjorie said.

Standing far back in a grove of beach and cedars, a large house was discernible, though not a human being was visible till Capt. Jenkins, with a voice calculated to awaken the echoes, if nothing more, shouted a far reaching "halloo," which the distance had scarcely swallowed up, when an answer came back to them, "halloo-o-o," and in a moment more a couple of negroes stood upon the sandy shore, waving their tattered hats in salutation. Disappearing for an instant, they soon reappeared and paddled toward the tow, in

a couple of "dug-outs," somewhat cautiously at first, for the sight of Yankee soldiers
was to a degree terrifying, but they were
soon reassured and paddled up alongside.
Hugh explained that they had horses aboard
and wished to get water. "Yes, sah; yes,
sah; plenty watah, sah ; wud de gemmens go
show, see de priests, day five or six ob 'em
wen dey all home, lives in de big house yon-
der." The "dug-out" is neither a capacious
or remarkably stiff craft, and its manipula-
tion calls for the exercise of skill and prudence, so Griswold and Olmstead cautiously
seated themselves, one in the stern of each
boat, and were paddled ashore by the negroes. Approaching the house, they espied
a priest, an elderly, handsome man, pacing
up and down, evidently in deep meditation,
but the moment he saw his visitors his face
brightened, and approaching them, he extended his hand and bade them welcome.
Turning, he led them into the house, intro-
ducing them to a large room furnished in
mahogany in the most sumptuous manner.
Sofas of curious carving, inlaid with pre-

cious woods and even metals; chairs with carved legs of animals and a sideboard which was a marvel of workmanship of the time of the Renaissance; the front seemed to be in imitation of the facade of a cathedral, arranged with the most curious drawers and cabinets, an article of furniture which had come down through the ages, priceless in value, dark and mellow with the influences of time.

Hugh stated the business which had brought them to shore, and their affable host placed every convenience which the place could boast at their disposal and, as they turned to leave, with thanks for his kindness, he approached the sideboard and opening a cabinet in the left hand side, took therefrom a large black bottle and some glasses. "This," he said, holding the bottle up, "is never empty. The key of this cabinet hangs *here*," pointing to a brass hook at one side. "Help yourselves *now*, and as often as you like during your stay; so long as you remain—the slender resources of our house are at your service." He explained to

them that there were a number of them having their home there, that it was the headquarters of the brotherhood of St. Mary's
County, but that their duties kept them most
of the time from home; that he had but just
returned himself, to hold mass in their little
chapel on the morrow, and would then be
off again, but that they were to make themselves at home; the housekeeper would see
that they wanted nothing. With thanks for
his kindness and the promise to see him next
morning at mass, Hugh and Olmstead set
about getting water to the barges. With the
assistance of the negroes, they formed a
good sized raft by lashing four dug-outs together, and covering them with boards and
placing a couple of barrels on it, which they
filled, they succeeded in relieving the fam-
ished animals. But it was a long and tedious task, and night had effectually closed in
before it was accomplished.

The wind had died out with the setting of
the sun. The moon was riding high in the
heavens, and on the waters, within the dark
shelter of their little harbor, the star-beams

rested like firefly lamps, and the deep, black
shadows of the tall beeches, following the
contour of the shore; the stillness unbroken
save by an occasional strain of vocal music,
from a negro's cabin deep within the woods,
or the cry of a water-fowl further up the
stream; the faint gleam of a light from between the shutter of some window in the
good priest's house; the puffing of a steamer, shooting by upon the water of the broad
Potomac; the neighing of a restless animal
in the hold, stole upon the senses in weird
expression of the reign of night.

Long the party sat upon the deck. Hardly a word was spoken. The impressive
beauty and peacefulness of the scene, the
sense of security from the perils of the restless bay beyond; the sweet, welcome calm
which had settled upon the earth; the low,
soft murmurs upon the evening air; stirred
within the heart of each one of them, some
tender memory, or, in quiet, self-communing
they invoked fruition of a treasured hope.
But the shadows along the shore were deep-
ening; the moon was falling lower and pre-

sently would sink to rest, far beyond the
fringe of timber, out among the cresting
waves. Within the priest's house but a single window let out a beam of light upon the
night; the good man was perhaps deep in
meditation or in prayer. Softly Olmstead
slipped down into the cabin, reappearing
with his guitar, and presently, upon the air,
there stole the sounds of music. Sweetly
over the waters, on through the thickening
gloom, faintly echoed from the distant
reaches of the woods, chiming in, perhaps,
with the good man's own thoughts or muttered prayer, came the sound of that sweet
invocation to the Virgin:

"Holy mother, guide his footsteps, guide them at a
moment, guide them at a moment sure."

And e'er the song is o'er the shutters are
thrown wide and reveal the occupant of the
room, his white hair streaming, his bowed
head glorified in the flood of golden light and,
as the last notes die away, he extends his
hands toward the little bay, and in a deep,
rich voice sends to the singers his blessing
from the distance : "Benedicite ! Amen," and

quietly, as the shutters close upon him again, the party separates and night draws her curtains closer and all is still.

The next morning the travelers were up betimes intent upon attending early mass, to which the circumstances surrounding them lent a romantic interest. The day was warm and bright, or promised to be. As yet, the horizon disclosed but the tints of dawn, but the air was balmy, the wind had completely died away, the storm had passed and left but faint suggestions of its stay.

Upon the little raft the party reached the shore where they found the good priest waiting for them, and under his guidance they set out for the chapel. Standing upon a gentle rise of ground beyond the fringe of timber which almost hid the home of the brotherhood, looking out upon the long stretch of sand, washed by both the waters of the river and the bay, embowered within the cool shade of a clump of cedars, the little building, constructed in the form of a cross, stood with open doors, an invitation to the weary to enter in. A little organ, long untouched the priest told them (for the war had sadly broken in upon their customs and form of worship), stood at the far end of the building opposite the altar. Madelaine asked if she might open it and play, " Our party is a passable quartette and, perhaps, we may revive the old-time impressions of the service."

The priest was enchanted at the idea, and very soon the low, plaintive strains of the Voluntary, a selection from Chopin, fell upon the air, drawing the worshippers through the mystic influences of its sweet spell nearer to the throne of God. Lower and lower the organ's melodious voice spoke out the accents of adoration, then died away and left its faintest echoes upon the ear and its benediction of peace within the heart. Seldom, even in its day of greatest glory, had the walls of the little chapel echoed the accents of sweeter voices; never, for years to come, should they know the like again. "This day will be to me a golden memory," said the priest to Marjorie, "later on, I shall hear your voices, even when you are far away."

Breakfast was enjoyed at the priest's house, the table being laid in a large dining-room facing upon the river, a room wainscoted and furnished in oak, its massive appointments speaking of a day long gone by—the imperishable monuments to a wealth and glory which had yielded to the agencies and exactions of relentless war. A horse and chaise stood at the porch, and, consigning his visitors to the care of the old woman who acted as housekeeper, the venerable man took his leave shortly after, wishing them "God speed" upon their voyage, and a blessing upon their after journeyings through life.

It was still early in the day, the men from the barges were busy watering the horses again, and Madelaine and Marjorie wandered about the roomy old house, admiring its quaintly carved furniture, its pictures and bric-a-brac; wondering how so many beautiful and costly things had found their way into the possession of a band of priests who, from the nature of their roving lives, had little time to enjoy them. But that mystery was never solved. The old housekeeper, though kind and attentive, was as a sealed book concerning the traditions of the place or its occupants. Seating themselves upon the veranda overlooking the river, they looked out upon the moving panorama with a fascinated interest. Several steamers, loaded with troops and bands of music, passed down on their way to the rendezvous; a vessel with low, rakish smoke-stacks and showing some threatening guns, seemed hovering about with no apparent object be-yond observation ; a few white sails out upon the bay flapped lazily in the fitful breeze. Nothing could induce Mr. Hale and Captain Jenkins to join the party in their early start from the boat; but, now, the young ladies spied them coming ashore on the raft, Mr. Hale not over-confident and the Captain in evident enjoyment of his discomfiture. " A regular catamaran," he called out; "beats any-thing I have seen since I was in the South seas." " Why did not Mrs. Jenkins come ashore, Captain ?" asked Madelaine.

" Wal, you see, Miss, the old oomans a bit

timid like; she says she yielded a pint in stepping aboard the '& Ru Jaxn' and she'll go no further. She said this raft might do on a pinch but it was no pleasure boat, so she staid behind."

"Then I shall go back and stay with her," Madelaine declared, and so indeed she did, leaving Marjorie to pilot the new comers about the place. But Olmstead had other views regarding the occupancy of Marjorie's time. He had secured a small, flat-bottomed skiff from a negro some distance up stream, and soon appeared with an invitation for that young person to accompany him upon a voyage of discovery, so these two started off and were soon lost to view. To the men aboard the barges, this Sunday was a day of feasting; the negroes came alongside with dug-outs filled with delicious oysters which they piled upon the decks, and which the men, seated about in groups, enjoyed to their heart's content, and these, with some fine fish they caught, gave them such a banquet as they had not enjoyed for many a day. Madelaine, upon reaching

the barge, brought Mrs. Jenkins upon deck,
and as she sketched the little harbor and its
surroundings, the elder woman gleaned much
of her companion's troubled life and her kind,
motherly heart went out to her, as though
she had been her own, and to Madelaine
there came a peace beyond anything she had
known for many a weary day, and she wondered afterward if what Mrs. Jenkins had
said could indeed be true. "You're going
to mourn so, lassie, there's a bright day coming, poor thing, and may be not far off. God
seems sometimes far away when he's close
at hand." And the two women sat long together in silence. To them both, sorrow
had come out in a different form. To one,
the song of life was nearly ended. The
cadences which fell upon her ear were low
and distant; memories chased each other
down through the vista of the long years
past and now, passed on hand in hand with
the hopes her faith had given her toward the
end. To the other, there had been a sudden
stop—a rude breaking of a string which
stilled for the moment the rhythmic story life

was telling, but for her, the goal was distant. Now, she was walking amidst the shadows ; would the sunlight ever struggle through?

Olmstead, having secured Marjorie to himself, bent to the oars till a curve in the stream hid them from view. Then he took to the duties of his position more leisurely, and together they idled along through the windings of the little river, stopping now and then to land, while Marjorie gathered a pretty fern or some rich and tempting mosses, and once they pulled up to talk to some little negro boys who were fishing upon the bank, and whose bright faces and laughing eyes effectively dispelled some of the gloomy ideas of slave life which had haunted Marjorie ever since she had entered this southern country. But their Arcadian voyage was brought to an untimely end by the admonitory signals of their tug's whistle and the cries of human voices and as they rounded the little curve which discovered to them their anchorage, there was a stir and bustle aboard, betokening preparation for a move. Shooting alongside, they learned that the Captain had concluded to push on—the sea had calmed down, and he would make a night run of it to Fortress Monroe and so, everybody being collected, the tow strung out again and headed for the bay. To the left of them, as they quit the river, lay Point Lookout, with its many buildings and tents, the site of a large hospital over which gracefully floated the National colors in evidence of military occupation, and in their onward course the features of the landscape faded one by one away, and looking back, the tree-tops in the little grove where there had been dispensed to them so gracious a hospitality, nodded to them as though imbued with the spirit of the good priest's words: a Godspeed upon their voyage.

CHAPTER VI.

The bright morning sunlight was scattering the mist which, like a ghost had settled upon the waters, disclosing the outlines of Fortress Monroe and the shadowy forms of vessels lying at anchor within the Roads, as the little tug, puffing and laboring with its heavy burden, steamed along towards its destination.

Upon the parapet of the Fort, groups, here and there of men intent upon watching the strange incoming assortment of craft, seemed dim and distant, and many a glass was leveled at the travelers aboard the " & Ru Jaxn," as they stood out on deck in enjoyment of the scene. Passing near the long wharf, activity was apparent everywhere—boats unloading men and munitions of war; huge piles of shot and shell; a few long, threatening-looking guns, lay to one side with gun carriages and field pieces—the thousand and one articles entering into the

impedimenta of an army. Sentries paced
here and there, gangs of laborers, a babel of
voices, an officer or two superintending and
giving orders, and in the background, the
huge fortress, the muzzles of innumerable
guns visible in the embrasures; the green of
its slopes in soft and pleasing contrast with
the grey of the stone and the white shining
sands at its base. The little park at one side
was neglected and deserted, save by a few
birds which skipped about through the
branches in the enjoyment of the sunlight;
the picturesque effects of pretty women and
uniformed men, had passed into memory;
the cosy seats were broken or in decay—the
only voices upon the air were laden with
the deeper tones of men—the pleasant
aspects of the place were gone—pleasure no
longer held its revel there.

Hugh pointed out the places of interest to
the ladies as they steamed along—the distant rip-raps—the scene of the encounter
between the huge and dreaded Merrimac
and the despised Monitor—the Norfolk
Navy Yard far over the waters and, as they

looked, the little steamer ceased its struggles—the swish of the water along its sides
no longer told the story of its progress; before them, a long strip of white, shining
sand, bordering a far-reaching level plain,
proclaimed their journey's end.

"Oh, Mr. Olmstead," exclaimed Marjorie,
"we are really here. I am so sorry; why it
has been a perfect dream from beginning to
end."

"Yes," said Olmstead, "and will yet be to
me for many a day."

They were standing a little apart from the
rest, and Olmstead felt as though the end of
all things was at hand. Impressionable at all
times, he felt himself in the meshes at last;
he saw no escape, nor would he have wished
any, but he resolved to dream his sweet dream
so long as he might; if there was to be an
awakening he would put it off so long as
he could and Marjorie, seemingly unconscious of all save the novelty of the situation, the busy scene before her, the influences
of her surroundings, gave thought to these
things alone; the *present* held enough to

claim her attention, she had no need to borrow of the future.

Griswold's camp was established on a pretty, sloping stretch of green, a quarter of a mile back from the river bank and between two knolls, separating it from the long lines of tents at either side, and hiding it away from some of the disagreeable features of a large encampment. Toward its establishment, Hugh and Olmstead had been busy since they landed. The ladies had stayed aboard, getting together their belongings and maturing their plans for the future, but Griswold had them promise to stay a couple of days in camp at any rate, and having plenty of canvas, preparations were made for them accordingly.

Toward evening, they strolled over to the landing again to assemble their party, and say "good-bye" to Captain Jenkins and his wife, and take a last look at the craft, upon which they had passed so many pleasant hours, and which was to put back immediately to resume its inland voyages. There was a feeling of sadness crept into every

one's heart as the time came to separate, for
they had received much kindness at the
hands of the plain old salt and his good
spouse, and there seemed no likelihood that
they should ever meet again, and it seemed
like the beginning of the end of an agreeable experience, each one of them would long
remember. But the "good-byes" were
spoken at last, and the "& Ru Jaxn," with her
owners, passed, as in a moving panorama,
from view.

Everything which the scant resources at
hand admitted of, had been done to make the
camp comfortable, and upon the tent de-
signed for occupancy by the young ladies,
Olmstead had expended all the fertility of
his genius.

Immediately after supper, which Flynn
had prepared for them, Mr. Hale, with Griswold and Madelaine, had gone over to hunt
up the mail, and Olmstead and Marjorie
strolled about the camp, looking at the
horses and the guns, and admiring the in-
genuity with which the men were making
themselves comfortable in their new quar-

ters. " Are you not glad to get into camp again, Mr. Olmstead?" said Marjorie. " And do you suppose you will ever get things straightened out?"

" Glad? No. I cannot say that I am. Getting into camp means drill and hard work again and besides, *you* had no avenue of escape while we were aboard the boat, and *now* the world is before you and you will be leaving us."

" Quite naturally," said Marjorie, "though traveling under military escort is simply fascinating, and I should love to prolong it, but that seems impossible. Have you ever been to Fortress Monroe, Mr. Olmstead?"

" Yes; but never in its days of social glory," replied Olmstead. " There are traditions clinging to the old Fortress and its surroundings that would fill many an interesting page. In the olden times, before the war, when it was a sort of border-land between the north and south, where many an army man, northern born, received his first impression of the influences a tropical sun exerted upon the habits, customs and man-

ners of life of those born and raised beneath
it ; where, perhaps, for the first time, he came
in contact with a social condition so entirely
different from anything he had been accustomed to ; where the self-reliance of *one* section, met the dependence of another, and the
fascinating languorous characteristics of the
southern women, contrasted with the animated, impulsive freshness of their northern
sisters in a charming and effective picture, it
probably combined more features of attraction than any other point on the American
continent ; certainly it was the " Mecca " of
all who sought a middle ground, between the
extremes of climate."

" Yes," replied Marjorie, " I have always
known Fortress Monroe as a place where
' *the season* ' never ended, the termination of
one was but the commencement of another,
but what is it like now ? "

" Given over to the prosaic entirely, I
fancy. There is little poetry centering
there now, except that of its traditions
and future possibilities. Whenever a
place becomes a base of military supplies

or operations, there is but one aspect to
its character; it is full of suggestions of the
cruelties and barbarities of war. But my
latest recollection of the place is associated
with a little hospital experience which I am
not likely to forget." "Do you mean that you
were ill at the hospital?" asked Marjorie.
"Why, yes," said Olmstead, " a classmate
and I lay upon adjoining beds for three days,
without recognizing each other. We both
had camp-fever contracted up *that* river
there," pointing to the " James," which was
on their right, " but we were just fresh from
West Point and couldn't stand much then.
The worst part of it was the sound of shuf-
fling feet at night, as they carried some poor
fellow out who had died—how on earth does
your sister stand it, Miss Marjorie? She must
see all kinds of sad and unnerving sights."

"Really, I cannot tell, but she says that all
she thinks of is how she can relieve suffering.
If she *sees* the horrible things it is only with
eyes which are seeking for a remedy. I
never could do it; I wish I were more like
her; I wish I were good for something, but

I do not believe that I am; not in such times as these, at any rate."

"To which statement I enter a solemn protest," answered Olmstead, "A young lady who can win the heart of an old salt like Captain Jenkins and absolutely subdue the native exuberance of that savage, Flynn, has not lived in vain."

"No, the discovery that one's sphere is an humble one is sufficient compensation for having lived at all, if nothing more," retorted Marjorie, with a suspicion of asperity in her voice. "Oh, you will make me quite vain, Mr. Olmstead. Is this what you are pleased to call subtle flattery?"

"Flattery! no. I merely wished to express to you the fact that you possess the power of humanizing even the most refractory subjects. I should call that a merited compliment, not flattery."

"You are a person of very nice distinctions at any rate," replied Marjorie, who really had become very fond of Olmstead, but who liked to invent situations for the pleasure it afforded her of witnessing his methods of extricating himself.

"I do not think it requires extraordinary discernment to discover that you are the loveliest girl in all the world, and, Marjorie, why should I not tell you now what you must know already—that I love you—I have loved you all along, ever since that first night when we sang together, and the good old priest, standing by his open window, extended his hands and sent us his blessing, and, do you remember, that for an instant the moonlight struggled through the trees and rested upon us, as it is resting now? I prayed then that it might be a happy omen. Has it found fruition, Marjorie?"

Standing upon the river bank whither they had wandered, Marjorie looked out over the waters. Vessels of every kind were riding there at anchor, the lanterns in the rigging showing plainer and plainer as the moon sank lower to her rest; far out toward the sea stretched a broad white shimmering line of sandy beach; upon the plain behind them, the canvas city rested peacefully, gleaming in the fitful light of its thousand camp-fires; the "God of Peace" had spead his wings athwart the scene, and in Marjorie's heart there awoke an answering echo to Olmstead's spoken prayer, and turning toward him she gently laid her head upon his breast, and, as he pressed her to his heart, the moon yielded up its vigil of the night to the silent stars, and

" Sank o'er the ridge of the world."

CHAPTER VII

After Hugh Griswold had left the "Academy" there was a marked change in the aspect of every accessory of the ball, from Kitty Wilmerding's standpoint. Before she had known of his being there, before she had been so forcibly brought face to face with the happenings of a year ago, and Hugh's words—though pleasant to her ear at all times, like distant echoes of a bygone day—had suddenly overleaped the barriers of time and rung out again with all the force of their true significance; the ball had seemed to her a scene of fairy enchantment. The music, the embellishments which gave setting to the graceful beauty with which the scene was peopled; that mystic splendor with which the night revealed her glories to the dying day; the subtle sense of power with which she, as queen of her coterie, was invested, had exercised the spell of forgetfulness to all beside. But he had come and gone; his manly voice had spoken her name; and in its tones were the accents dear to every true woman's heart; and now, before her, uprose that parting scene, when he, obedient to her will, had gone from her to brave new dangers, taking with him but the shadowy substance of a hope which she had but feebly sanctioned. About her was the same glittering throng; on the air, the sweet music rose and fell like waves upon the ocean, in soft, rhythmic, undulating measure, but to her ear it was as the roar of breakers upon a rockbound shore. The words which gallant men whispered to her, the laughter rippling round, had lost their charm, their spell was broken, she was listening for a note which was upon the air no longer, and the rest were out of tune. When at last she was alone within the security of her own chamber, and had divested herself of ornament and gown and gently laid aside a bunch of roses which Hugh had brought to her, and seated herself upon the rug before the glowing coals to comb out her golden hair, she dreamed the sweetest dream of all her life.

"Dear Hugh," she muttered, "and I let him go again without a word, and I love him so." And the night wore on, the coals were dying in the grate; the first beams of day were creeping in through the the parting of her curtain; before rousing herself from her reverie, she crept into her soft, warm bed, and with the new-born joy in her heart, forgot the world and all her weariness.

It was late when Kitty awoke. For some time she lay, turning over in her mind the events of the night past; picking up the train of her thought where she had dropped it, when sleep had overtaken her. Mingling with the outside noises of the city, there seemed to come to her distant strains of music, the tones of voices confused and indistinct; a babel of sounds which sleep had only stilled for the moment. The scenes of the ball were before her again; the panorama of glad faces and bright eyes and sparkling jewels; the subtle odors; the whispered compliment; the graceful undulations of the dancers; the whole witchery and bewilderment of the scene; yet, amidst the pleasures of the momentary retrospect; amidst the intangible memories of the night's impressions, there came to her inmost consciousness the revelation of her heart's faith and yearning love, of the man who had honored her above all other women, and from out of the shadow of her irresolution and uncertainty there came at last, struggling into the light, the form and substance of what had before been but vague and indistinct. She had only the bitterness of self-reproach replying to her self-questioning of why she had sent Hugh away again, without the promise that he asked, and, would he come again? she kept repeating. It seemed all so strange to her, this feeling that within *one* being lay the power to make or mar her happiness forever; it was all so sudden of discovery that she was almost inclined to doubt its truth; but some inward voice kept whispering it to her heart; the ticking of the little clock upon the mantle kept repeating: "I love him, I love him, I love him;" it seemed as though at times she could hear, too, her own name spoken, and

that the speaker's voice, was his. Lightly
she sprang out of bed, and peeping between
the curtains looked out upon the day. The
sun was high above the tree-tops. A flood of
light gilded the cornices of the dwelling opposite her own; the vane of a distant church
steeple glistened as a ball of fire in its reflection against the cloudless sky; people were
hurrying to and fro; a long line of school
girls at regulation pace, went calmly by; the
busy hum of the city's life smote upon
her ear. Turning from the window, she began
to dress, idling through the task in a dreamy
fashion, unlike her usual self. Standing before her glass, combing out the heavy braids
of golden hair, she looked at her reflection
long and critically. She had been told often
enough that she was beautiful, but never by
him did he deem her so; she wondered.
Poor little Kitty! how suddenly the knowledge of her own heart had been followed by
an attendant train of speculations, as to *her*
own claims to preference, before the hundreds
of *other* women, to whom she had conceded
charms she had never arrogated to herself.

Life had ever been to her a burst of glorious sunshine; she had been too busied with the beauty of all things surrounding her to turn her thoughts back upon herself; but now it was all different. She valued the loveliness which spoke to her out of her mirror, as fit setting to the life which she was ready to place within her lover's keeping, and her long scrutiny seemed happy of result, for, as she turned away, her face was all alight with a sweet, contented smile, as though her soul stood within the open doorway of her eyes, answering back the questions they had asked. Kitty's was not the beauty of a girl city-born and bred, nurtured amidst luxurious surroundings sheltered from every rude blast sweeping by; hidden from the warmth of sunlight; blossoming amidst night's poisonous counterfeits of day; the beauty of the "Calla" suffused in borrowed glory. Hers was the beauty of the wild rose, bestowing its fragrance upon the hill-side; mingling its own delicate hues with the heavy bloom of clover; listening to the whisperings of the meadow brooks; drinking in the freshness of the wandering winds and the dews of the morning. The mountains were home to her; she knew the voices of the forest, and they had often echoed back her own; she had grown up familiar with summer's verdure and autumnal dyes. Often, as a girl, she had climbed the mountain side overshadowing her pretty home, and sat for hours upon some mossy rock, or lain in the grasses sweet with heather, looking out upon the world beyond, whither the river, far below, was trending; wondering what it all was like, weaving the fancies of happy girlhood, while the leaves overhead, rustled soft music in the breeze which tossed her hair into waves of shimmering gold, and bore along the seeds which sprung to roses in her cheek. The world was all a beautiful playground to her imagining; the contrasts of weary toil and poverty and crime were sealed books to her understanding; the waves of disappointment and despair had never dashed their strength on the shimmering sands of her Arcadian shore and, as girlhood yielded its faint suggestions to the developing influ-

ences of maturer years and the dreams of
yesterday, became memories of to-day, there
shone through her eyes a sweet and gentle
spirit, innocent of the shock of any rude
awakening.

Her toilet completed; her form enveloped
in the soft clinging folds of a pretty wrap-
per; her hair caught with a dainty ribbon
and falling in a shower of curls upon her
shoulders, a single half-opened bud of a
"Meteor" rose nestling on her bosom; she
drew back the curtains of her window and
stood looking out upon the street below,
when a gentle knock at her door brought her
thoughts back from their wandering, and the
next instant, her sister came into the room.

"Good morning, dear; why, how sweet you
look! one would hardly suppose you had
been out all night; come, now, and have some
breakfast and tell me about the ball." And
Mrs. Farnham came over to where Kitty
stood, and put her arm about her and drew
her toward her and kissed her, as she always
did, upon her forehead. "Was it all you
locked for, Kitty?"

"Oh, it was lovely," answered Kitty, "I could never have fancied anything quite so beautiful; but I was glad when it was all over." And the attentive ears of her sister detected a little sigh, rather out of keeping with Kitty's accustomed enthusiasm, and, quick to take alarm, she asked:

'What is it, dearest, are you tired out? or what is it makes you sigh?" and she looked into her sweet, fathomless eyes and thought she detected a troubled look in their liquid depths; but Kitty smiled and said that she was very happy; that perhaps she *was* a little tired, and it would pass.

But Mrs. Farnham knew her sister too well to be deceived. Something had happened and she must know what it was. Kitty was intrusted for the time, to her keeping, and she loved her beyond anything, next to her own children. If she were unhappy, she would try to help her. So together they went to the pretty, bright breakfast-room, where some blazing logs were throwing a grateful warmth upon the air. In a bay window, revelling in the sunlight, were fuchsias

and geraniums, and a plant or two of helio-
trope and hibiscus, and looking down upon
it all, warbling his matin greeting, a canary
swung upon a perch within his gilded cage.

It was as cozy a little room as heart could
desire and made for confidences. Its influences were all inspiring. The genial
warmth; the shaded light; the soft contrast-
ing colors; the subtle perfume. A sweet
nook in fairy land where two lovely women
might pour out to each other heart-secrets
which would not be out of tune with their
surroundings. Whatever it may be in
woman's intuition which quickens a suspicion into the full flower of conviction in matters wherein the heart is affected; whether
instinct, or drawn from education or experience, or the outcome of some subtle com-
munity of womanly thought; or a prescience,
born of faint, undefined suggestions of manner or of speech; whether the recognition of
outward sign, or an inward consciousness—
the secret of a woman's love, guard it jeal-
ously as she may, will, in some moment of
forgetfulness, reveal itself and to Mrs. Farn-

ham, the revelation of Kitty's new-born tenderness, came quick and sudden.

Kitty talked incessantly when once they had seated themselves, describing the ball; the costumes; the accessories of every kind which added to the beauty of the scene. She spoke of Blaisdel and a dozen other men, of every one, in fact, but Hugh, trying, through volubility of talk, to hide the real crowning feature of the night's development, but she achieved a questionable success. She had not given credit to her sister for any depth of penetration; still Mrs. Farnham let her talk on, knowing full well that in due time the confession would be made. Later in the day some flowers were brought to Kitty with Blaisdel's card and a penciled hope that she "had not succumbed to the night's exactions," and while they brought her pleasure as everything beautiful did, they had no meaning to her, beyond the graceful expression of a kindly thought; she valued the bud resting upon her bosom far above them all, albeit *they* were sweet and fresh and *this* half withered. Kitty was happy in the thought that Hugh loved her; her happiness had come to her gratefully as a perfume sometimes steals upon the air before one is conscious that the flower exhaling it is near— sweetly as out of the stillness a strain of music voices—soft accompaniment to one's thought; but a feeling came with it all which she had never known before, an undefined dread, a restlessness she could not control. Nothing seemed quite the same; a voice seemed calling to her out of the past; the dream of her hitherto happy, careless spirit had passed into the awakening of reality; the wings of her fancy, which had hitherto born her along, heedless of the way she took, now seemed guided by some unseen hand directing her toward an unknown goal.

The days passed by, one following the other in uneventful procession. Men came and went, performed their little graceful acts of devotion, and passed by again. She walked and danced and skated, but in a perfunctory sort of way—the zest was wanting. She felt at times as though she must fly away from it all— fly back to her beloved hills.

Their voices were ever sweet upon her ear; *they* were tangible and immutable, not vague and transitory as were the things entering into the city's life. At last one morning Hugh's letter came, brought into the room as they sat at breakfast, and Mr. Farnham tossed it over to her with some remark about: "A letter from the front for Miss Wilmerding," and as Kitty took it up she felt the eyes of her sister upon her and the warm flush upon neck and brow, which made speech unnecessary, in betrayal of her secret. Without a word she read her letter through. Mr. Farnham had left the room and she and her sister were alone, and going around to where her sister sat, Kitty placed the missive in her hand, and with her arm about her neck, kissed her, as she said:

"Read it, dear; you must like him for my sake, for he is to be my husband."

And then closing the door gently behind her, she found in her own room that which caters to a woman's need, whether in joy or in sorrow—solitude and tears.

CHAPTER VIII.

The next day was a busy one at Newport News. The morning light which forty-eight hours before had crept over the tree-tops and lain unbroken upon the broad level stretch of land bordering the woods, now outlined the shadows of the tents and wagon trains and of the active life so suddenly settled down upon it; the tapering spars of vessels lay reflected in long dark lines upon the water; the reaches of the far off, opposite shore, were low and indistinct, but within the limits of the camp was a scene of boisterous and aggressive life. To the ladies of the party, the camp was a source of unfailing interest—the workings of the military mechanism, a matter of wonder, and to Marjorie it was altogether past understanding, how men, cooped up as they were within the limits of their little tents, gave such evidence of contentment, singing and chatting with an animation suggestive of a careless happiness, forgetful of

past and indifferent to prospective hardships
or dangers.　Marjorie and Olmstead strolled
about the place taking in all the varied scenes
presenting themselves, wandered over to the
river bank and through the booths which speculative traders had erected there, loitered
along the beach, watching the vessels at anchor or others moving through the sparkling waters; the "men of war," tugging at
their cables in the moving tide; talking of
their future, as they listened to the story the
rippling waves were telling to the sands.

Later in the day Olmstead contrived to find
a saddle for Marjorie and mounting her upon
his own horse, a handsome bay, they rode
out to look at what was once a lovely village
nestling amidst shady trees whose branches
moved in the soft southern breeze which
warmed into life flowers and fruits of many a
hue and flavor, and invited indulgence in that
languorous "far niente" existence, which
only a southron knows:—Hampton, a pretty,
peaceful hamlet, through whose shaded streets
fair women in accessory of dainty fabric and
sparkling gems were wont to pass, while on

the air, the soft music of their voices lingered
and around them crowded the evidences of a
careless and luxurious life, now lying a mass
of charred and shapeless ruins, a damning
monument to the rancorous hatred and un-
pardonable charlatanism of a Confederate
commander. Scarcely a house was standing,
only a few, wretched negro hovels, upreared
amidst the ruin which lay outspread at every
hand. It was a sight to make an angel weep
and wring a curse from every feeling heart,
upon the desecrations and barbarities of war.
Marjorie sat for a while in silence, looking
down upon the ruins, wondering what had
become of all those who had been driven
away—shelterless, homeless, perhaps friend-
less ; looked down upon the seamed and scarred roadway stretching on into the heart of the
once peaceful and beautiful country, which
now lay shorn of everything which made it
once so fair, over which great armies had
marched and the din of battle thundered,
while many a spirit winged its flight into eternity and many a waiting woman learned that

the footfall for which she listened had passed
beyond her hearing.

It was dark before they found their way
back again to camp. At a headquarters,
near by, a band was playing an inspiriting air;
groups of men were standing about, listening
to the music, smoking and chatting gaily;
the lights of the vessels sparkled upon the
waters, a gentle breeze, coming from the sea,
laden with odors of sea-grasses and bordering
marsh-lands, stirred the canvas city into
shimmering, wavy undulations while the
shadows danced in weird array and the voices
of the woods beyond joined in the common
revelry. To Madelaine, the change of scene,
the separation from contact with misery
and suffering—the freedom of thought and
action—the balmy air of this warmer climate,
were already producing their effect. She
was more buoyant of spirit, the color was
coming back again into her cheeks, her eyes
were losing that fierce, unnatural brilliance of a
suffering thing which had so touched Hugh's
compassion ; she was being drawn, through
the agency of her surroundings more into

the current of the lives of those about her. Between Hugh and herself had grown, in those few days, a friendship in which each recognized strengthening influences, and in his long and earnest talks with her, she had found material for a more hopeful scheme of life than ever she had looked for. She had entered upon the work to which she had of late devoted herself in the frame of mind of one to whom all earthly joys were at an end —the iron of a bitter disappointment had eaten into her very soul.

The thought of any possible change, of time's healing power, had never come to her —but now, loyal as she was to her beloved dead—treasured as was the one memory which haunted her in her waking hours and lay upon her heart during the long dark hours of the night, fitful gleams of light fell upon her pathway—here and there a star shot its way through the darkness of her firmament, life had other duties, she began to recognize, than those of a despairing submission to a cruel fate, and with light came hope, and with hope the dawn of peace. It was to be their last

night in camp and it was late before the lights
went out in their several tents. Marjorie and
Olmstead had been busied with matters
touching their own future interests, but they
had kept their secret to themselves and the
stars looked down upon the camp that night
and twinkled merrily, as the soft winds mur-
mured a lullaby, and to the happy and the sad-
hearted alike came the sweet benison of sleep.

Several weeks have passed, Captain Griswold's battery has long since lost its visitors;
the pleasant time of recreation has given
place to the stern exactions of prosaic duty
and Newport News is again the scene of
active embarkation. Hugh has received his
anxiously looked-for letter and many others
have come to emphasize the promise Kitty
Wilmerding had given, and Olmstead, to
whom Hugh's happiness is a subject of re-
joicing, has not been forgotten. Hugh has
asked him no questions but quietly drawn his
own conclusions, "The youngster will tell me
in his own good time," he has thought, as the
mails came in, and side by side with his own,
was a delicate, perfumed missive for "the

boy " as well.   A large, side-wheeled steamer
has been devoted to his battery and the
horses are ranged in stalls upon the decks,
the guns occupying the inner spaces.   The
men are quartered about as convenience suggests and they steam out one beautiful morning down the Roads, skirting the long stretch
of sand-beach, and plunge into the deeper
waters of the Chesapeake; ho! for Baltimore.
Hugh and Olmstead saw little of each other
during the day.   Each was busy getting his
belongings together for the longer journey
beyond Baltimore, which would probably be
a time of separation from their trunks, and in
writing letters to drop into the mail when
the steamer landed. After supper they sat
together on the forward part of the steamer's
deck, talking over the events of the past few
days, speculating a little upon what kind of
work lay before them and often, during a
silence of greater or less extent, wreathing
fancies or dreaming dreams, as the smoke
from their cigars floated out in fragrant
clouds to mingle with the odors upon the
ocean air. Between these two men a very

warm friendship was established. Hugh, much older than his lieutenant, a man who had stood the buffetings of many years of service, matured in thought, of a quiet dignity of manner and yet a kindliness of speech and action which invited and inspired confidence while it repelled familiarity, stood in "loco parentis" to the young man who had only left his "Alma Mater" a year or two back, but who gave promise, with all his free, impetuous ways, of a future development worthy of the name he bore. Olmstead loved "Old Hugh" as he spoke *of*, but never *to* him, and would have gone far to serve him and farther still to have spared him trouble on his account, or disappointment. He looked up to him as a man who had weighed most things in the balances and knew the value of them. He always went to him if perplexed, certain to get the key of disentanglement of his troubles from his friend; he had seen him under too many circumstances not to fully know and appreciate the true metal he was made of. And now, as they sat in the cool evening air; the waters around them brilliant in

the rushes of phosphorescence as the waves
upreared their crests and then broke into a
thousand foam-flecked, disordered masses and
spread out upon the sea like a fall of white
blossoms upon dark green grasses; the som-
bre outline of the distant shore a bank of
gloom upon the background of a cloudless
sky; a shimmering band of light, far reaching across the waters, heaven's dower, upon
the " silver flashing surges " of the deep ; the
weird unnatural voices from out the night as
the winds swept through the cordage; the
throbbing of the engines in their tireless monotony, the sweet fresh odors released by the
night airs from the land and born to them
upon the breeze, the cry of the look-out breaking in upon their silence as a light flashed
out ahead in signal of some other vessel speeding toward them upon the sea's highway.
Olmstead broke in upon the current of Hugh's
thought with the rather vague statement :

"Captain, I can't keep it any longer—I
want to tell you something."

Hugh, half turning his chair and removing
the cigar from his mouth, blew forth a dense

cloud of smoke, slowly, as though giving Olmstead time to recover from his startling announcement and then helped that young gentleman through the embarrassing first stages of his confession, by the remark:

·" My dear boy, I thought you did, and I wondered how you kept it so long."

" Why, it hasn't been very long since it happened," replied Olmstead, wondering how Hugh knew anything about what he was going to say.

" Not as time is reckoned in ordinary matters I admit," exasperatingly answered Hugh, " but do you know you have shown more pre-occupation in the past few weeks, than in all the months we have been together and I have suspected it all along."

" Suspected *it !*—suspected *what ?* " cried Olmstead, who imagined his secret beyond the ken, even of so shrewd an observer as Hugh.

" Why, that you had something to tell me," said Hugh; " you have, haven't you? you said so just now ;" and Hugh, whose first impulse was to help him out, thought better of

it, seeing, as he did, that such a course would
be disappointing.

"Why, of course I have, and something
very important, to me, at least," replied Olm-
tead. "It's about Marjorie."

"Oh, about Marjorie, is it," answered Hugh.
"A lovely girl," he continued, as though in
soliloquy "and her sister, poor thing, my
heart has ached for her ever since——"

"Yes, so has mine," interrupted Olmstead,
"but I want your heart to *rejoice* just now; I
want you to tell me that Majorie is the sweetest girl in all the world and offer me your
congratulations, for Marjorie and I are to be
married some day."

Hugh rarely yielded to an impulse, but he
did on this occasion and got up from his seat
and laid his hand on Olmstead's shoulder and
looking down into the younger man's upturned face said:

"With all my heart, boy—she *is* a sweet
girl indeed and deserving of all the love you
can lavish on her—may God spare you to
come back for her. Ever since I have suspected it, I have felt my responsibility of you

increase a thousand fold, but if we only do our duty in life, He will take care of the rest." And Hugh sauntered off and looked far away across the waters over the bow of the boat and, mingling with his thoughts of Olmstead and Marjorie, was one of the fond, happy time, coming to himself as well:

> " Some sweet day
> Bye and bye,"

and presently coming back to where Olmstead sat he said:

" Now get out the box, youngster, and play something, it will do us both good," and, as later on, the sweet strains of soft, low music fell upon the air and the pilot up above from where they sat lowered his window, that the monotony of his watchfulness might be broken by some other sound than the rattle of the steering chain, and the watchman out in front, looked back for an instant in grateful greeting of the melody, Hugh thought he understood more perfectly, how the tones of " Fairthorn's " flute had fallen upon unhappy " Guy Darrel's " ear and softened the disappointments of his life.

Some ten days later from their camp at Lexington, where they had arrived the day before and settled down upon the outskirts of the pretty town, where already the buds were bursting and the green grasses were bedecked with the earliest flowers of spring, a letter found its way to Marjorie, detailing some of the happenings of their trip.

*　　*　　*　　*　　*

" I thought I missed you enough to have of itself satisfied any demands of a retributive justice upon me for the sins of my past life, but it seems that I was mistaken. From the moment we touched the wharf at Baltimore, began a series of mishaps and adventures the culmination of which I dread to contemplate. In the first place, in getting the animals ashore the plank broke as Duke, my beautiful bay, dearer than ever to me since you rode him, was being led off and he fell into the water and, as he had been feeding and still had his nose-bag on, he drowned before anyone could reach him, though half a dozen men jumped in to save him. I am afraid I must confess to having shed bitter tears as I saw the lovely fellow stretched out upon the sand and knew no power could give me back the faithful creature again. He and I had stood some hard knocks together and I had thought that some day he would be turned over to your gentle ministrations with no other calls upon him save those which *you* should make; but now that dream is vanished, and I shall never speak your name to him again as I have done every day since you left, or see the intelligent gleam in his eye as though he understood. I had him buried away from the crows and all the other vile things which make common prey of the bodies of the dead and the hearts of the living, and felt when the train rolled us away that I had turned my back forever upon a friend.

"Our train was quite a large one. The men and horses were placed upon box-cars, but the guns, etc., had open flats. About midnight one night as we were rolling along through the mountains a sudden violent commotion brought us upon our feet, and the train to a standstill; I was Officer of the Day, and jumped out to see what the matter was.

I found one of the poles of a caisson had come loose, and had smashed against the roof of a tunnel. So I went forward to have it fixed, and then gave the signal to start on. When our car reached me it was going at such a rate I could not get aboard, and there I was. Away the train thundered, leaving me alone at dead of night, the sole inhabitant, so far as I could see, of the mountain. The night was very cold. I had left my overcoat aboard, and had on my sabre and pistol, so I struck out along the ties with only the stars to light me on. After walking about an hour I spied way in the distance a light which took me another hour to reach. It proved to be a small section house, or way station, for no where in particular, simply dropped down there for the accommodation of any wayfarer who might happen to find himself in that be-nighted region, and desired to depart from it. The agent was up and looking over some books as I entered, my sabre clanking, awak-ening echoes which had never awakened be-fore, and instinctively he reached for his shot-gun. But I explained the situation to him, and ascertained that an express would come along just before day, but would not stop, which was very comforting. I could not get a train, he said, till sometime next day. But I made up my mind that the express *would* stop, if I could accomplish it, so I sat talking with him till I heard the train coming along, thundering through the mountains, shrieking at the curves and the mountains resounding with the noises far and near. I waited till the sound got near enough and then seizing the agent's lantern, I sprang out upon the track and signalled "down brakes." The agent swore eloquently, and the conductor joined in blasphemous chorus as the train came slowly to the station ; and before putting down the lantern I signalled " go ahead again," cried out " good night " to the agent and jumped aboard. I overtook our train at Grafton, and just in time, too, for a few moments after we were bowling along for the Ohio river, at Parkersburg.

" Now we are camped on the outskirts of one of the prettiest little towns anywhere, with promise of lively times in a social way.

Kentucky people have always been famed for their hospitality, and I doubt not, under the humanizing influences surrounding us here, our savage state will undergo material modification.

"Dear old Hugh is kind and thoughtful as ever, and in his quiet way seems so happy, now that his engagement with Miss Wilmerding is an assured fact. You do not know, though, that after you left she wrote him, in answer to a letter of his, giving him the promise he asked, and he never seems to worry any more. I could not help telling him of *our own* engagement, and felt so much better when I had done so. He seemed so glad, and said he felt an added responsibility regarding *me* now, as though for *your* sake he must needs look after *me*, which I thought quite complimentary to me at any rate. I have never known a man in whom selfishness was so absolutely impossible as in him.

"Our destination is as yet unknown, though probably we shall stay somewhere in Kentucky for some time to come, and I think we can stand it after all we have been through.

"Here, at Lexington, we find a queer admixture of the Union and Rebel sentiment—the Union predominating, however, I think; but there is nothing rancorous, as I have seen it elsewhere, and whatever bitterness exists is concealed beneath a courteous demeanor. Though we have been here only a couple of days we know half the town, and shall doubtless know the other half before we go."

*   *   *   *   *

There was much more in Olmstead's letter; but let us draw the curtain before those expressions of tenderness to which he yielded, as became the existing state of things between those two. There is a sacredness in certain utterances which it were sacrilege to look in upon.

But Captain Griswold's battery was not alone upon this pleasant scene of action. Troops were encamped in considerable numbers within easy distance, and the staffs of one or two headquarters were there to share and dispute with them their claims to the generous hospitalities of the people, and so it happened that, following a time-honored custom, the officers, desirous of returning in some measure the attentions they had received, made arrangements for a ball. The most conspicuous talent in that direction which their numbers possessed was employed for a fortnight before the event was to take place, in the artistic arrangements of the hall and every incidental of the fete. The resources of Cincinnati as well as Lexington were taxed to no inconsiderable degree to meet the exigencies of the occasion. The products of hot-houses and the open ground were levied upon to make a fit setting to the bright gems of sweet womanhood which should grace the scene. A famous caterer had carte-blanche in his own peculiar province. A military band and cotillon orchestra were to alternate with inspiriting airs and dreamy inspirations to rhythmic measures. Light and garland, banner and festoon, shrub and flower; soft shimmering drapery and emblazonry of bar and star, were invoked in the creation of an earthly paradise;—a neutral ground over which Euterpe and

Terpsichore flung the spells of their enchantment, and the little winged god, through the
agency of a subtle power, disguised the bitterness of political creeds within the enfold-
ing of his mantle, as he whispered to willing
ears the story to which all the world has
listened. Lexington had been placed in
singular straits, but had borne herself with a
dignity and graciousness toward both the
opposing factions, as the fortunes of war
placed her in alternate possession of them.
There was no manifestation of exuoerant
sentiment for *either* party. It had been a
graceful submission to the penalty of a geo-
graphic position which made the people of
Lexington respected by North and South.
Personal interest was subordinate to personal dignity. There was no outcry against
fate or the rude exactions of military necessity. However strongly men felt, they seemed to recognize the fact that their destinies
were being shaped by stronger hands than
theirs, and bravely awaited the issue. Lexington had given her *sons* to both sides in the
contest; was it matter of surprise that her

daughters' hearts were filled with love and sympathy for the cause of the absent ones? To their credit, be it said, the gentleness and modesty of woman was never disguised in the bitterness of partisanship.

At length the night rolled round, a cloudless, warm delicious day, filled with the song of birds and odors from fields and wooded stretches; with sunshine lurking everywhere, on housetop and the reaches of the wood; coaxing the meadows into bloom and fragrance,throwing shadows which peered above the fences or lay upon the soft blue grasspatches, or in moody silence watched the sunbeam's caress of some fair face, which, from a casement looked out upon the fresh beauty of the spring; a day wherein the questioning voices of all nature sounded sweetly on the ear, and the "winds set free the answers of the trees and the shrubs," and to which the dying sun at last lent tints of purple and of gold, as fitting garb wherewith to greet the night, and she, in shimmering, silvered vestment, bedecked with diamond stars and the glory of a softened radiance, threw the spell of her enchantment upon the earth.

And now, within the ball-room, there was the murmur of happy voices, mingling with the soft, seductive strains of music, and a flood of light from a hundred colored lamps suffusing all the scene, as though in the borrowed beauty of the "after-glow"—the rustling of silks, like the voices of the winds amidst the reeds within the marshes ; the shimmer of satin and accessory of pearls ; the soft tints of many clinging fabrics ; the simplicity of lawn and tulle with the embellishment of buds and flowers ; the undulant motions of the dancers, like waves upon the sea ; bright uniforms, with glitter of gold and the scarlet contrast of silken sash ; the delicious abandonment to the spells the hour unloosed, were there to emphasize the revel.

Olmstead thought he had never seen anything quite so beautiful. It was like a chapter from a fairy book, indeed, and he almost feared the coming of an evil genius to throw the spell of disenchantment and awaken him from a delicious dream.

He was sitting in one of those deep windows which afforded a safe retreat from the rush and whirl of the crowded room, the sash was thrown open, the soft evening breeze gently fanning the glowing cheeks, and stirring a truant tress of his fair companion's hair. They had been talking about the war, and of how its cruelties had come home to so many in the quiet town; of how the old-time traditions were being effaced in the new order of things, following in the train of passing events; of the sudden change from a life of pleasure and activity, to the tedious one of waiting, and Olmstead had been led from generalities to talk of some personal experience, when the clanking of a sabre attracted their attention, and looking round, they saw an orderly approaching with a note. Olmstead took it and read:

"Come to camp for a moment. I have sent your horse." H. G.

"What is it, Mr. Olmstead? Nothing terrible, I hope," said the young lady, as some one came in at the same moment to claim a dance.

"I cannot imagine," he replied." "Captain Griswold was not feeling well to-night, and so did not come to the ball; perhaps he is ill; I must go.'

"But you will return: you promised to tell me of Fortress Monroe, which has always been the Mecca of my hopes. I shall look for you, so do not disappoint me."

"Not if I can help it," said Olmstead? "the flattering thought that you will even hold me in remembrance will speed my going and hasten my return." And bowing low before her, Olmstead turned, and springing lightly through the window, was soon lost to sight amongst the shrubbery. A few moments later he rode into camp, and throwing himself from the saddle, entered Griswold's tent.

"What is it?" he asked.

Griswold was busy packing a valise, and without a word, handed a telegram to him to read, and Olmstead read;

"Kitty very ill. Come."   FARNHAM

*   *   *   *   *

CHAPTER X.

Several days after Kitty's disclosures to
her sister, Blaisdel had come to take her to
see a famous picture then on exhibition at one
of the galleries of the city and together they
had gone out into the glory of the winter
afternoon, with its flood of sunlight and crisp
cool air, on which the pleasant jingle of sleigh-
bells rang as the handsome turn-outs upon the
avenue dashed by. They threaded their way
through the throngs upon the streets, meeting
and nodding to acquaintances here and there,
chatting of a hundred things just then the features of attraction, looked in at the windows
made gorgeous with costly fabric or banks of
hot-house flowers or marvels of the gold-
smith's art and eventually passed in, through
the outer gallery, to an inner one where the
picture they had come to see was hung. Perhaps a dozen people were there in wrapt attention of the striking canvas. A woman and
a man were standing upon the shore of the

sea. Her face was sad and full of apprehension. Her head rested upon his shoulder and he was looking down into her upturned face upon which the light fell so that it was half hidden in shadow. The lips were half parted, as though she were drinking in all he was saying. Hope seemed struggling with a dread foreboding. The man's face was dark and handsome and full of energy, but there was a tenderness in his look that spoke all the intensity of his passion for the woman. A vessel lay at anchor in the offing. Upon the shore the waves were tumbling in white foamy masses,

> "And while he kissed her fears away,
> The gentle waters kissed the shore.
> And sadly whispering, seemed to say;
> He'll come no more, he'll come no more."

This seemed to be the inspiration of the picture. Pathetic as was the subject, the coloring was sublime and the drawing and perspective faultless, and in *these* lay the artist's power.

Kitty sat and looked at the picture for some time without speaking, indeed the sound of a human voice then would have seemed out of place to her. In the study of the painting she was in some way, she felt, in spiritual communion with its author, for pictures to her were but mirrors of the mind, as blossoms are symbols of the gentle, tender thoughts of woman and too, through some subtle association of ideas, that parting scene spoke eloquently to her through memory of another parting, wherein *she* was an actor, and a sad-faced *man* another. And then she gazed, in dreamy, absent fashion, as the gentle current of her thought flowed on, and a tenderness took possession of her heart and unconsciously her lips and voice gave form and accent to a name, which, falling on the stillness, startled her out of her reverie and told Blaisdel the secret she had not meant to tell. For an instant their eyes met and then, moved by a common impulse, they strolled out into the larger room—Blaisdel with full knowledge that Hugh had won and that his own hopes were vain and Kitty, with a tell-tale color in her cheeks and a light within her eyes, which told that *she* was not ashamed.

For a few moments they mingled with the

crowd, admiring a gem as it fell beneath their
gaze, or mildly criticising an inferior subject
till, at last, Blaisdel turned to her and said :
" May I congratulate you Kitty? or would i$_t$
be premature ? "

" Not premature, I think," she answered·
" Has Hugh never spoken of me to you ? "

" Yes, in a general way. Any *knowledge*
I possess, however, comes by inference,
rather than by any assurance of his ; certainly he has not told me of his good fortune.
You will not care if I write and wish him
joy ? "

" If so you regard it, certainly not," she
answered. " I had thought the more grateful heart should have been my own."

" Charming," replied Blaisdel, " might I
venture an inquiry as to *when* Hugh's happiness was assured to him ?'

" It was assured to him when, after returning home from the 'Charity Ball,' I fell upon
my knees and prayed to God I might be
worthy of so generous a heart as his. It was
promised to him yesterday. Do not offend
my happiness by your sarcasm, Charlie ;

surely we have been too good friends for
that, and I have been vain enough to hope
that we would always be."

Blaisdel was cut deeper than he himself
suspected. He had gone on flirting with,
half-loving, first one and then another, but
imperceptibly, quite unknown and unsuspected by himself, Kitty Wilmerding had thrown
around him, all innocently, the influences of
her charming personality; tendrils which
had laid hold of his susceptible but fickle
heart more strongly than he knew. But
now, as the voice of duty bade him lay hold
of her image and tear it from him, he felt
how hard it was. But his was a nature not
devoid of good or of generosity. He never
would be untrue to his friendship for Hugh,
nor pain Kitty, by pleading a cause he plain-
ly saw was lost.

"Pardon me, Kitty," he said. "I would
be a churl indeed to withhold my congratulations to you both, and your friendship will
be ever dear to me in the future, as it has
outrivalled any other in the past."

And so they went out through the crowd

of loungers into the street again. The winter
day was drawing to its close. Shadows
lengthened across the roadway. The tide of
humanity was moving homeward. The air
was chill and the sleigh bells rang out in
shriller tones. There was a chrystalline brilliance in the salient points which caught the
last rays of the sinking sun. Footsteps fell
upon the stone pavements with a sharp, crisp
sound. High riding above the world, a cold,
pale moon was set in the clear vault of
heaven awaiting the dying of the day and
the hour of her own glory. Kitty drew her
cloak more closely about her as they were
born along by the irresistible living tide.
Once or twice she shuddered, and Blaisdel
asked if she were ill, but she thought not.
She was only chilly and her head pained a
little, and so they walked on till her sister's
home was reached and Blaisdel left her, glad
to be alone with his own thoughts again.

But Kitty *was* ill. That night a high fever
set in and the hours dragged on slowly—
tediously. She heard the solemn tones of
the city clocks within the steeples ring out

the record of the time upon the frosty air.
The roll of a passing carriage in muffled
accents fell upon her ear like the muttering
of distant thunder.   The little night-lamp
threw all the appointments of her room into
confused and uncertain prominence, and the
shadows rested like weird, unnatural visitors
across the walls and the hangings of the
chamber.   Strange forms peopled the scenes
upon which her distorted fancy dwelt. Often
she started as though in terror, and then re-
lapsed into the fevered sleep of exhaustion.
The next day her fever had increased; the
doctor's medicines were impotent to quell its
raging.   Except a low, unintelligible muttering which at times showed the struggle of
her mind against her malady, she lay with
closed eyes, waiting.   Another day, and the
doctors shook their heads in foreboding;
slowly, but surely, she was yielding to the
deadly nature of her disease.   Hugh's name
was upon her lips, and fell upon the listening ears at frequent intervals; her thoughts
seemed all of him.   Blaisdel had sent her
some handsome flowers, which rested near

the bedside, and on them her eyes would
rest a moment and then upon her sister, with
a look of inquiry, followed by one of pleading and she was understood, and her sister
kneeling beside her and taking her little pale
hand within her own, whispered: "He is
coming, dear," and a glad, grateful light
would beam a moment in her eyes and she
would doze off again more peacefully, happier apparently, than before. All that skill
could do, all that tender nursing could accomplish, her faithful, loving friends bestowed, yet daily the sweet girl's life drew
near to its end. Realizing it, she accepted
her doom without a murmur. Of herself
she had no fear, only for Hugh was her mind
troubled, and only for him a sorrow lay near
her heart, to which the tears which coursed
down her cheeks at times gave mute, pathetic
emphasis.

And so she lingered on—she had loosed all
claims to earth save one, and *that* she could
not yield—her unwavering faith in God's
mercy made death impotent to draw the veil,
before her eyes should rest once more upon

the face of the man she loved, before his
arm should lift her weary head upon his
breast, and as life's accents faded, his voice
should be the last to linger upon her ear as
she passed beyond into the rest and beauty
of the spirit land.

CHAPTER XI.

When Olmstead read the telegram which Hugh had handed him he stood for an instant dazed. The tidings of illness, followed so quickly on the heels of that happy, exuberant health, which, as exemplified in Kitty, had given promise, in connection with the tenor of her letters, of so much future gladness, that he could not reconcile the two. Hugh did not speak. Speech seemed impossible, in presence of this dread message. Mechanically he hurried his preparations for departure. A train left at midnight and e'er morning he should be far on his journey.

"Hugh," said Olmstead, and the name fell from his lips with an unfamiliar sound, for it was the first time he had ever addressed him so, "**Hugh, dear old friend, how can I help you?**"

"Boy," said Griswold, "there is but *One* that can help me now—pray for me as you never prayed before,—and for her," **and his** great, sad, kind eyes had a hopeless, piteous look in them as he continued: " It is hard to be brave and loyal to one's faith in such a presence as this, one never knows what sorrow is, till it comes home to him in this wise," and he wrung Olmstead's hand as he turned to go. " Take care of things till I come back," he added, "it will not be long, *in any case*," and Olmstead choked down a great sob as he caught him in his arms and the tears streamed down his cheeks, as though a *brother's* crowning sorrow cried out to him for pity and for love.

The receding rattle of the ambulance wheels sounded fainter and fainter as Hugh was rolled away to the station. Olmstead stood out in the night, beneath the quiet stars, looking into the shadow of the woods beyond his camp, and thought, as they lay so close to the golden moonbeams which flooded the bordering meadow-land, how typical they were of the dull realities which linger near life's poetry—how it was but a single step from out the light of hope and faith and glad anticipation, into the darkness

of despair and desolation. He had no mind
for a continuance of the gayety, the sound of
which came faintly to his ear; the undulating
inspirations of the orchestra, sounded hollow
and unnatural in their commingling with the
dull thud of this new-born revelation of an
appalling possibility. He wrapt himself in
his cloak and seated himself before the tent, following Hugh in his thoughts and, as Hugh's
words came back to him : " Pray for me as
you never prayed before," he fell into mute
communion with that great Spirit who alone
can save, and at whose throne he felt he was
now standing, a suppliant, side by side with
his heavy-hearted friend.

Two days later a train thundered into the
station, as New York was awakening from its
sleep. The flush of the nascent day was
spreading above the horizon across the river
and the wooded hills beyond; the rumble of
the city's noises were breaking in upon the
stillness which had boded above the outspread
miles of housetops, and towering spires, first
to catch the summons, lit up the beacon-fires
as heralds of the coming golden flood. The

sharp shrill voices of the Arabs of the street
hawked yesterday's record of the pulsing
world to every passer by; into the long, far-
reaching avenue the by-streets poured the
tribular waters of their living tides; deep-
voiced, with loud clang and quivering rever-
beration, iron tongues proclaimed the hour;
the grey mists, like baffled ghosts, receded,
and the triumphant march of another day,
began.

Over the stony streets rattled the carriage
which Hugh had hailed to take him to a
hotel, where he might remove the stain of
travel. The sharp click of the horse's hoof-
beats sounded unpleasantly upon his ear;
they seemed to him to be singing out the
knell of all his earthly hope, and he breathed
more freely when they stopped. Springing
out, he secured his room and made all haste
with his toilet.

"What if it be already too late," and great
drops stood upon his forehead as the cruel
thought flashed across his mind.

Presently, as he again went out, the clerk
noticed the pale, sad-faced man, and his

active brain began to invent the cause, and
he whispered to his fellow "some trouble
there," and then, whistling softly, he turned
to his books and arranged the business for
the day, and forgot the misery just now
passed out into the street.

Hugh had not far to walk. In a few moments he saw the drawn curtains of the
house he sought. Upon the pavement in
the roadway, saw-dust was spread to deaden
the sounds of travel. " Thank God no crape
is on the door-knob," he muttered, and the
light of a blessed hope fell upon his heart,
that perhaps the struggling young life within
had conquered.

The door swung open obedient to his light
summons. Evidently he was expected, for
Mrs. Farnham was there to receive him.

" Come," she said, " thank God you are in
time."

Hugh followed her mechanically up the
heavily carpeted stairway noiselessly, as one
treads in the presence of a great calamity.
His heart seemed to cease its pulsing; the
weakness of a terrible fear came over him;

he felt that he stood upon the brink of a sacrifice greater than he could bear. A moment later he stood beside the pillow of his loved one. Her eyes were closed—a poor, wan hand lay upon the white spread, a thing of wax, with faint tracery of blue, as a thread shows in the petal of a flower—the long lashes of her lustrous eyes rested uneasily upon the sweet pale face; the dim light of the room shaded the lines which illness had carved on brow and cheek, hiding the cruel contrast to her erstwhile radiant beauty.

Hugh dropped upon his knees beside the bed, and tenderly took the little hand in his, and bending over the prostrate form, spoke her name. A quivering of the eyelids, a little twitching of the sensitive mouth, a sigh, faint as a distant woodland echo, and the sweet eyes opened; a smile of happy welcome, a whisper of his name, and as the curtain for an instant gently parted, a ray of glory fell upon them—heaven's golden emblem of the pledge of love, registered beyond the skies.

"Dear Hugh," she whispered, "lift me, let me look out into the sunshine once more, there let my head lie upon your breast. I am happy now; kiss me, dear. See, Hugh, the great white doors are opening; do you not hear the music, dear Hugh?" and her head rested more heavily upon his breast; the dear eyes closed; a smile, as though in glad answer to a happy summons parted her lips and her spirit was gone—flown back again to the God who had loaned it to make beautiful an earthly tabernacle

All that was left of sweet Kitty Wilmerding was laid away to rest amidst the shadows of her beloved hills, but their voices would no more answer back her cry, or glad birds voice the chorus of her song. The strings were broken; the harp was stilled; faded flowers lay upon the pathway which the agile feet had trod; there was a sigh among the mountain pines for

> "The eyes that smile no more
> The unreturning feet."

Hugh Griswold stood alone upon the mossy slope. Beneath the waving branches which overshadowed her resting place, the last rays of the setting sun lay slanting across the peaceful scene, and along the silent streets where the grasses grew, which harbored blue-bells and daisies and sweet violets in the summer time. Now, the blight of winter lay upon the earth, but its mutterings were growing feeble; there was a presence in the air which was herald of the spring. Far down below, the shining river rolled its tide onward along the valley. Faint sounds of life struggled up the steep incline in profanation of the quiet of this city of the dead. Silent and sad, looking far off beyond the limits of the gathering gloom, the sunlight faded from off the earth, as every joy had faded from out his heart. Struggling with the cruel thoughts of God's injustice he stood and, as

> "Through his heart the tremor ran
> Of grief that cannot weep,"

he reverently knelt beside the new-made grave and peering down, as though the hidden upturned face were revealed to him again, softly spoke her name, feeling that in

some way she would hear, and, as at last, in
infinite relief to his pent-up agony, the tears
streamed down his manly face, he spoke
aloud ;

> " My love was weary ;—
> God bless her, she's asleep,"

and turning toward the world again, he took
up the burden of his life and sadly and
silently passed on.

Griswold returned immediately to his battery, arriving at Lexington in the early afternoon of a warm sunny day. There was nothing now to have kept him in the east ; he
could not have born the idleness which an
extended leave would have imposed. He
wanted activity and hard work ; the harder
the better, anything to take him away from
himself. He carried with him a memory
which was dearer than anything the world
had in its offering. But he felt that it must
have its place, he could not keep it before his mental vision, hour after hour, day
after day. Only when the day's work was
done, and the stars were set in the sky estab-
lishing the reign of night, did he give himself
over wholly to his thoughts of what might

have been, and the cruel reflection of what was.

On his westward journey he had stopped for a day at Mr. Hale's home, more for Olmstead's sake than his own; even in the midst of his own bitter sorrow, he did not forget "the boy" he had left behind, *He* would be glad to hear of Marjorie from one who had seen her face to face; for himself, he desired to bespeak for them a happier outcome to their hopes, than had been vouchsafed to him; there was that in the man's nature which never made it possible for him to yield wholly to consideration of self.

Madelaine he had found better in every way. Change of scene, contact with brighter things, had softened the cruelties of her disappointment; she looked upon life more hopefully, but nothing could swerve her from her determination to go again to the hospitals when she was a little stronger; therein lay the work she had assigned herself; therein she would labor, so long as woman's nursing could avail.

"I am so sorry for you," she had said to

Griswold, "but I know how feeble words are
in such a case as yours. Try not to live too
much in the past; look ahead, as you bade me
do. Thank God that at least you have a
noble work to do, and from out the future, as
you enter it upon the path of duty, there will
come to meet you, inspired, perhaps by her,
not Lethe's tide, but the gentle, rippling
stream, within whose depths are the waters
of Nepenthe."

With "the boy" his meeting had been an
almost silent one. There was an eloquence
in the way Olmstead threw his arms about
him and whispered: "Dear old Hugh," beyond anything else he could have spoken,
and Hugh was grateful to him for it, and so
together they took up the routine of their
duties, and often, as they sat before their
tents, in the soft light of the fading day, their
thoughts traveled back together and hovered
in tenderest memory above a little grave,
across which lay the lengthening shadows; but
they rarely spoke Kittie's name—it seemed
like a profanation of the silence, in which her
spirit dwelt.

CHAPTER XII.

Griswold's battery was not destined for a long sojourn in Kentucky's garden spot. The sweet spring weather had wrought a wondrous change upon the landscape and, enriched with leaf and blossom and the many shades of soft carpeting which lay unrolled, stretching far as the eye could reach, the whole country side was beautiful in the extreme. But other changes, which they were called upon to watch more closely, were occurring upon less peaceful and inviting scenes of action, and Griswold had not long returned from his sad journey to the East, before they were off again, for Vicksburg. But of their participation in that campaign, the struggle against hardship, and exposure and oppressive heat, and the low fevers of the bayous and the marsh-lands, the gradual investment of the city, its resistance, and ultimate surrender, this narrative has nothing to do.

Midsummer had passed, and September

suns were tempered to the husbandman and the dwellers in canvas cities as well. Kentucky's harvest time was drawing to its close, and already the night airs were chill, and tints of royal gold and purple were showing upon the hill-sides and within the meadows.

Lexington had awakened from her sleep of summer; the quiet of her streets was invaded by cavalcade and market caravan. On stated days, the Court House Square, a scene of barter and of sale, revealed the varied products of the soil and beasts of noble pedigree; the denizens of country-side and city, fraternized upon the common plane of reciprocal dependence.

Griswold's battery was a daily scene of activity; it was getting into shape again, after the ordeals of its recent campaign. New men and horses were being drilled; needed repairs and replenishment of ammunition and supplies were being attended to; preparations for yet another campaign were being pushed to completion.

In a quiet way, Hugh mingled with the hospitable people of the city, and to Olm-

stead there was a never-ending whirl of ex-
citement: lawn and riding parties, dinners
and dances, excursions to various suburban
places of attraction, music and sweet dalli-
ance, the poetry of life, after contact with its
more material aspects, and it was little wonder, that when the morning of that dull day,
late in September dawned, which saw the
battery strung out upon the road, headed for
the Cumberland mountains and Knoxville
beyond as their objective point, that his brain
grew dizzy in the effort to locate the *exact*
abiding place of his susceptible heart.

But they filed along, out past the awakening town, past the outlying pretty residences
with their groves of historic oaks and neatly
kept lawns; out beyond that atmosphere upon which lay the incense of beauty and of
bloom and around which would ever cling
bright memories, till a turn in the road shut
away the city from their view, and closed another chapter of experience.

Their line of march lay along the rich,
cultivated fields of the Blue Grass region;
out through Nicholasville and Crab-Orchard,

and here, leaving the smooth macadamized roads, they plunged into the intricacies of the mountain passes, the rumbling wheels of caisson and gun-carriage awakening echoes amidst the shadows of the virgin forest, which rolled along the mountain sides like mutterings of distant thunder.

At last, after days of hard marching and struggling with nearly impassable roads, the heights beyond Knoxville loomed up before them—gaunt, staid sentinels, above the peaceful valley, which followed the curving of the Holston river far as the eye could reach. Long afterward, looking back over the scene in the light of his memory of it, as first it was unfolded before him, Hugh felt the cruelty of war's curse upon the land. The smiling landscape of his memory revealed the pretty town, built upon rolling hills, at whose base the Holston, in broad sweeping curve, freighted with the legends of the far up-country districts, which, dark in their deep, impenetrable vesture of wild laurel, lost form and contour in the purpling distance, lay like a burnished silver beam in the southern sunshine. High mountain peaks, in abrupt upheaval, dominated the fertile valley, which, in graceful, wooded undulations, stretched east and west through miles of farm-land and walnut groves. Outlying the city's limits, here and there upreared upon some salient point, stood low, rambling southern homes within the shadows of pines and cedars and the embowerment of clematis and honeysuckle and Virginia creeper, with stretch of lawn, and contrast of a thousand tints of bloom. Centrally, throughout the valley, the railroad wound its sinuous length along, annihilating distance. Now, the hills were bared of coverings. Scarred and seamed they lay, their peaceful, smiling aspect hidden in the rude transformations which marked the trail of war. A girdle of breastworks, yellow and forbidding, gave abrupt and ugly termination to the graceful slopes leading to the city's heart; the peaceful, outlying houses lay in smoked and shattered ruins, here and there a vine-covered wall, standing in ghostly mockery of a whilom scene of beauty and of thrift. Even God's acre, in its ruined aspect; its fences gone; its marbles broken; its pathways deep with furrow of screaming shell, looked up to heaven in mute appeal, from the cruelties and irreverence of man.

On the night of the 12th of November, Griswold, Olmstead and the battery surgeon were grouped about the little Sibley stove in their mess-tent, smoking their pipes and listening to the pattering rain as it fell, driven by the chill winds, upon the canvas. Until that very day the weather had been beautiful, but, at last, the much-dreaded rain had come and all knew what *that* meant should an order come to move. The Doctor, apart from his qualifications as a professional man, was a public benefactor to their mess. A German "jusqu'au bout des ongles," he possessed all the characteristics of his race—an indefatigable worker—an excellent cook, and one, too, who could evolve from *nothing* the most satisfying and savory dishes, good-natured and with a fund of anecdote, upon which he always drew liberally, when the spirits of his comrades lagged. On this particular night, he was busy with a " brew " of his own invention, a " Sphirit varmer," as he called it (and it was no misnomer), and had just delivered himself of the remark, " Vell, poys, I hope ve don't get ordered oud in dot rain," when the clattering of a horse's hoof-beats caused them all to exchange hurried glances. A moment more and a tap on the canvas settled the matter in their minds.

" General ——— wishes to see Captain Griswold at headquarters at once."

" All right," said Hugh, and calling to Flynn for his horse, he was riding, a few moments later, up the road toward the town.

It transpired that a large Confederate force was moving up from the vicinity of Chattanooga, evidently with the intention of re-occupying East Tennessee and all the troops available were ordered post haste to Loudon, thirty miles distant and at the railroad crossing of the Tennessee river to oppose it.

Griswold was told to get on the road as soon as possible, and to march with all dispatch, and report to the General again, when

he should reach Loudon. The rain was falling now in torrents, the night was pitch dark
and the lanterns of the sergeants as they
moved about superintending the preparations, threw a dim spectral light about the
camp. At last, as the first suspicion of daylight made the road visible, the battery rolled
out of park and headed down the road.
There was no abatement of the storm, the
wind blew in furious gusts driving the cold
rain peltingly into the eyes of rider and
horse, there was not a dry garment in the
entire command, but they dragged along,
over the slippery hills, through the deep,
boggy lanes, making cut-offs through the
fields where the roads were too heavy. On,
on, animated with but one desire, to be in
time. With short intervals of rest, they plod-
ded on during all the day, and into the night,
till the utter darkness made further progress
impossible; then, they filed into a neighboring field and halted. It was with the utmost
difficulty that tents could be pitched at all;
the wind whistled and whirled about as
though bent upon destruction. At last,

after much hard work, their tent was up: they pitched but *one*, it was no time for luxury, some place to lie down and rest was all they wanted. An hour or so later, they had just ranged themselves round a mess-pan of a hot and tempting evidence of the Doctor's skill, when a sudden, mighty rush and whirl of wind lifted their tent completely from the ground and hurled it fifty feet from where they sat; their supper was overturned and, looking about them, the whole battery was a scene of desolation. Not a piece of canvas standing ; the poor horses with heads lowered and backs to the storm ; men running here and there, intent upon the recovery of some missing article of apparel, and confusion everywhere. Tired out, dispirited, seeing the uselessness of essaying to pitch the camp again in the yielding soil, they one and all wrapped themselves in their blankets (albeit they were heavy and wet), and lay down to sleep beneath the sodden sky, the shrieking winds for their lullaby.

At daylight they moved on again; the roads now were well nigh impassable, and

the pitiless storm showed no signs of abatement. Whip and spur were needed now to
rouse the tired horses to a last effort. The
fringe of timber marking the river's course
was dimly defined in the distance. Columns
of infantry were laboring along, now under
the partial shelter of the bordering woods;
now in the open of a cleared and furrowed
field; distant shots told of the enemy's presence; here and there a horse lay dead, a
victim of the urgent necessity of the hour;
a straggling soldier, taxed beyond endur-
ance, an abandoned wagon, a lost spur, a
broken wheel, a watchful vulture, sailing
amidst the scudding clouds, filled up the
spaces in the speaking picture.

At last, exhausted, utterly unable to much
farther drag their weary feet along, they
toiled to the summit of a little hill and saw,
outstretched before them, the plâteau bordering the river bank, and, as they gathered
themselves together for the short home-
stretch, a band, by the roadside, stationed
there by the Colonel of an Ohio Regiment,
struck up "Rally round the Flag." The

effect was marvelous—men and horses seemed imbued with a new and vigorous life, and
sprang forward as though the hard struggles
of the past forty-eight hours had dropped
from out the scale—the wheels rumbled
along as though impelled by unseen hands—
a shout, as though of victory, rang out upon
the air, and Griswold's battery rolled into
park—on time.

Griswold hurried off for orders to a group
of officers standing round a camp-fire not far
distant.

"Unhitch, but do not unharness your
horses," the General said, "we cannot tell
what may happen," and as he spoke, a shout,
short and shrill, which every Union man had
learned to couple with a dash against their
front, broke out; a rattle of musketry, the
answered yell as the attacking force receded,
and then the stillness of the grave. The
enemy was making a dash for cover on the
river bank.

Returning to the battery, Griswold gave
orders—first, for the horses' care; then, for
his men. "Get what rest you can," he said;

"pitch no tents; give the horses double rations; unlimber and reverse the pieces."

Flynn and the Doctor were grand that afternoon, and within an hour, a savory mess was ready for the starving party, which they dispatched with a relish that only a soldier can appreciate.

The rain had ceased to fall; the clouds broke away little by little; the distant horizon grew vague and purple; outlines lost their sharpness; stealthily the shadows settled on the wooded heights and crept down into the valley; the camp-fire's blaze was brighter; a few stars studded the darkling vault of heaven; night's reign had begun, and over the watchful hosts a stillness rested, ominous—oppressive.

Slowly the hours dragged on; men when they spoke, did so with voices which were low and unnatural; every sound that broke upon the air carried its impressions of significance. Roused from a restless sleep, men sat up and listened; from out the quiet belt of impenetrable shadow hanging above the river bank, none knew what might come;

the weariness, the suspense; the benumbing cold; the uncertain possibilities which lay concealed within the coming hour; the majesty of death foreshadowed in the mental tableau of the impending struggle, precluded restful sleep or needed rehabilitation. Midnight passed; the moon was coming up above the hills, and through the valley the silvery light painted grotesque images upon the ground. A cricket chirped from a protecting thicket; the distant voices of tree-toads, like mimic sleigh-bells, filled the air with christalline reverberations; a speculative owl hooted from a neighboring tree; weariness had gained the mastery over the restless host.

Olmstead, stretched out upon a board which he had picked up from a neighboring deserted house, was back again with Marjorie, the accents of her sweet voice were on his ear; he was drawing with her the plan of her future life; he felt the pressure of her hand; over his senses stole the influences of sweet communion; when, like a lightning flash, the dream vanished. He found himself upon his

feet, instinctively running to his guns.
The air was laden with the deafening roar of
musketry; the yell and shout of men in fierce
engagement. Like a roar of mighty thunder,
without a moment's premonition; sudden,
fierce, terrible, the din of conflict broke upon
the stillness; rolled over the valley; hurled
back in deafening echoes from the distant
hill-sides, startling into active life the sleeping thousands, and then, suddenly, as it had
come, the tumult ended; and, as the smoke
clouds rolled away, the stars looked down
from heaven in merry, twinkling mood, and
the moon set her silent, painted shadows
once more upon the earth. And so the night
wore on, a weary watching and waiting for
the day, with alternate attack and oppression
of silence. At last, about three o'clock, the
shrill notes of a hundred bugles rang out
upon the air; there was a stir and bustle, a
hurried breakfast, and long lines of infantry
crept over the hills, back on the same road
they had toiled over only a few hours before.
Wagon trains also took up the weary route
again, and batteries here and there dispu-

ted with them the right of way. So wretched
had the roads become, so deep and heavy in
the red, clinging clay, that trains were
doubled and scores of wagons, deprived of
locomotive force, were drawn close together
and with their contents given over to the
flames. High above the tree-tops the lurid
flames shot into the air, the artificial light
converting the dark hours before dawn into
the searching brilliance of noon. Projected
against the hill-side, the flashes of reflected
light from rifle-barrel and brazen field-piece
shimmered as gleaming moonbeams upon a
ruffled sea, and the creeping shadows lengthening as they receded into the distance,
formed a spectral panorama of night shapes
flying from the day.

And now the whole army is in route, only
a strong rear-guard checks the impetus of
the enemy's advance; mile after mile of
weary marching, the roadways lined with
stores deserted, to lighten the loads of the
tired animals; here, a wagon hopelessly
abandoned in some deep quagmire; further
on, teams quadrupled to drag a sunken gun

from the deep, bottomless mud. Solid columns and knots of stragglers; loose animals
and rejected harness; cries of teamsters and
crack of whip; curse and laughter; the occasional ping of a bullet speeding over head
the given and answered shot and challenge
of the rear and advance guards of the con-
tending legions.

Hour succeeded to hour—the sun had
crept on, steadily to the zenith—the morning mists had been long since dissipated and
a clear and cloudless sky over-arched the sodden earth. Steadily the enemy advanced; as
steadily the Union troops retreated, the des-
ultory firing of the skirmishers ringing out
upon the air voiced menace and defiance—
now and then a yell and deafening rattle of
musketry told of a charge to recover the
body of a fallen comrade; then the *occasional*
shot, proclaimed the slow advance and retreat. again. But the triumphal march of
battle is not the glittering pageant which
sweeps athwart the scene leaving its impressions of martial bearing and burnished arms
and waving standards and patriotic music.

The pæans of victory flash out upon the air and mingle with the voices of requiem; the laurels which crown the brow, give no token of the pall which enshrines the heart; the crimson blood which stains the earth voices the mighty sacrifice a nation makes, in honor's maintenance. But the reception tendered the aggressive visitors had lacked many of the elements of formality. The dispute of the river's passage had been made by a strengthened picket line, the forces of the opposing factions had had no test of their respective strength or metal. Surprise had not assumed the dignity of indignation, and now, through fifteen miles, with feebly muttered protest, the Union troops had retired and the moment had come wherein to check the fiery onset and double the advancing ranks back upon themselves. About two o'clock of the afternoon of this November day, the line of battle of the Federals was formed. The infantry following for the most part the line of a fence which ran perpendicular to the roadway curving backward toward the right; the artillery on the higher ground, behind.

Nearer and nearer came the sounds of the skirmishers firing—now they are nearly through the woods—a few more yards and the open, rolling ground in rear, discloses to our men the line of battle—waiting. Halting for a moment, they open a murderous fire upon their pursuers and then, with a yell and dash, reach the lines in safety. Quickly the opposing lines are formed. From the edge of the timber, guns protrude their muzzles; right and left the columns of infantry deploy, a struggling shot breaks in upon the stillness hovering above this scene of deadly preparation; a flutter of musketry, the occasional boom of a field-piece experimenting with the range, and now, a line of grey-coated men appears and with a bound and yell they have cleared the limit of the woods; down the slopes they come, their banners waving, the earth trembling beneath their heavy tread, the air resounding with the defiant iterating of that short, sharp cry, which was peculiarly their own, their cannon behind them hurling shot and shell into the Union ranks heralding their approach. But the blue-

coats hold their fire; nearer and nearer comes
the fierce human tide; our men can see their
features; now the whites of their eyes; and
an instant later, the groans of the dying, the
shriek of the wounded, the din of a murderous melting fire commingle, as the grey line
falters, halts and finally seeks refuge whence
it came.

The opening ceremonies had been performed; men of opposite creeds were strang-
ers to each other no longer; the battle of
Campbell's Station was inaugurated.

With varying fortune to either side the
conflict raged during that whole afternoon.
Once the Union lines retreated, but only a
few hundred yards, to a point of better van-
tage, and here they held their ground till
night closed down upon the scene and the
startled echoes sank to rest and the pitying
eyes of heaven looked down on friend and
foe alike.

But the night brought no rest to the tired
feet or wearied body or heavy eyes; the
Confederate lines were lapping over the
Union flanks and *they* must retire, or every

avenue of escape will soon be closed. Silently the worn out troops file into the road once more; horse and foot; battery and baggage-train; ambulance and ammunition wagon; the stars of heaven to light them on their way; the voices of woodland sprites, distinct above the whispered words of cheer, which pass from mouth to mouth; the groan of a wounded man, as a rough place in the roadway shakes his shattered body; the clinging mud adding extra strain to muscles almost overtaxed; no song to cheer; no shout of victory to linger on the ear and quicken the lagging pulse.

Late in the afternoon, Griswold had received orders to detach a section of his battery to report to the general, who was to command the rear-guard that night, and he had sent Olmstead, and the latter, crowded well to the side of the road, watched the retreating army as it filed along, a grim procession, through the shadowy forest; a weary, dispirited look in the eyes which had been innocent of sleep for forty-eight long hours;

half blinded by the smoke of battle, as the ears were half deafened by its din.

The pickets had begun their senseless firing again; even the boon of silence was denied to the weary hosts, and Olmstead, seeing the last regiment pass by, filed into his own appointed place, with a low word of command set his own little band in motion.

About midnight, the moon showed her face above the distant hills and peered in through the thick branches of the trees at the ghostly pageant.

A halt was ordered for ten minutes' rest; a regiment thrown back to strengthen the picket line and keep the enemy in check while this scant respite was enjoyed. The word was passed along the column in low tones scarce above a whisper and every soul of that weary column and every animal as well, dropped fast asleep before they had fairly settled down upon the ground. Olmstead threw himself from his horse and into a crotch formed by two displaced rails of a fence hard by and knew no more till aroused by the nearness of the firing and then, springing up, he took in his little squad at a glance. The horses nodded where they stood—the drivers had fallen forward on the necks of their faithful beasts and were far away, unconscious of their danger or the warning rattle so steadily creeping up upon them. The cannoneers lay wherever they had fallen—launched far amain beyond the sea of thought, upon the pleasant waters of a happy dream. No human voice could have roused those sleepers—yet, they must be up and doing. Seizing his orderly's bugle he shrilled upon the air the "Forward" signal and without a word of exclamation, a question or a protest, the fetters of sleep dropped off; each man and horse was alive again and moved, as though from out the shadow of the night, into the silvery shimmer of the moonbeams which lay across their path.

CHAPTER XIII.

By noon of the following day, the investment of the city was completed and Burnside's
little army cut off from communication with
the outer world and now, the work of des-
ecration began. Breastworks and redoubts,
batteries and abattis sprang up as though by
magic, and woe to lawn and grassy slope or
pretty dooryard which came in the pathway
of the line of defence; the exigencies of military necessity have little regard for nice distinctions and so the peaceful labor of years
in many cases faded before a single night's
preparation for war.

Griswold and Olmstead were located upon
the brow of a pretty little hill, the end of a
city street, which looked out over the country
through which they had first made acquaint-
ance with the natural beauties of the place.
Beneath them lay the railroad, with its neat
little depot beyond and near which had
sprung up a little village—an outlying feat-

ure of the city. Behind them, a small stone
Catholic church stood—its spire reared mod-
estly above the surrounding house-tops, its
gilded cross flashing in the sunlight, its sym-
bolized promise, far over the outspread scene.
A little school-house, deserted now of its
whilom occupants, graced a corner of the
churchyard. Far as eye could reach, to
right and left, lay the lines of the investing
army—closer and closer each dawning day disclosed their picket's rifle pits and few were
the intervals of rest; few the moments when,
upon the air, the ping of bullet or hoarse
scream of shell brought not a message of
menace or of death.

The November days were mostly bright
with sunshine, but the nights were chilly and
dispiriting. With insufficiency of clothing
and rations of the scantiest, with the mountain passes toward the east blocked with
snow, and sources of supply cut off, with suc-
cor nowhere visible, and the possibility of
capture looming up like a ghostly contingen-
cy upon the enemy's ability to keep closed
the gates to freedom but a little longer, men

with less of the true fire of patriotic spirit, less self-reliance and faith in their invincibility, might have found at Knoxville a speedy solution of the question of sovereignty over east Tennessee; but the troops throughout were cheerful. There was but little sickness, and an indomitable spirit of energy and determination supplied the place of numbers and resources. And so the time passed on, and the morning of the 29th dawned crisp and bright, besiegers and besieged quietly watching each other, and with little thought of the ghastly work in hand to darken the coming of another day. Early in the night the moon disappeared below the western hills, and impenetrable darkness settled down upon the earth. Somehow it was noised about that the enemy would attack sometime during the night, and preparations were made for his reception. Brush heaps, here and there, were fired before the Union lines to illumine the space over which the enemy would have to cross. At regular intervals of the night a shot went screaming down the railroad track, ploughing through

the air with voice of warning; men lay down
to rest with their rifles loaded and near at
hand—there was a portentous, mysterious
something upon the air, a sudden hush and
oppressive silence, a faint low murmur borne
at intervals upon the bosom of the gentle
breeze, pregnant with suggestion—and still
the night wore on—the pickets gave no sign
or token, the stars twinkled merrily in their
spheres, as though peace and rest were en-
throned upon the earth. But the storm was
gathering. A picket far in advance saw moving objects in the distance—now they drew
nearer—he could hear the low word of command—from the earth there seemed to rise a
surging on-coming ocean of humanity. Crack
went the warning rifle—another followed,
and others still, and then a yell, fierce, long,
determined—the yell of men who had left
behind them every thought save the single
one of grim determination " to do or die,"
and with a mighty rush they gallantly came
onward to their doom. And now the scene
was a lurid glare of light, the roll of musketry
trebled to the deep bass accompaniment of

cannon's roar; exultant shout and defiant
yell blended with groan and shriek of agony.
Over the slope, past the ditch filling with the
dead, well up the parapet, to the very muz-
zle of the guns, cheering each other on, victory seemingly within their grasp—the brave
Confederates came, but only to recoil before
the withering storm which made Fort San-
ders a wall of deadly fire, an impregnable
stronghold.   Again and again they breasted
that terrific storm.   It was a repetition of the
heroism and undaunted courage of Gettys-
burg—but it was as hopeless, and as the daylight crept above the eastern hills the shattered
columns withdrew and eternity's gates closed
upon the silent throng which had entered in
beyond sight or sound of earthly passions.

Griswold, lying beside his guns—a ghastly
wound upon the head—another in his side, was
to all seeming, dead.   They had *drawn* him
aside from the mouth of an embrazure where
he had fallen—out of the way of the struggling
mass of fierce humanity.   There was no time
for nursing or asking questions—a Nation's
credit—an army's life was in the scale.   When

the conflict ceased Olmstead knelt beside him
and looked down into the upturned white and
silent face—he bent his head to listen—"Thank
God he breathes "—but Hugh knew nothing
of the tenderness which bore him away from
the ghastly scene ; knew nothing of the gentle ministrations of those who loved him.
His low short breathing told that life was
not extinct, but the thread which bound him
to it was very slender—how long could it
stand the strain?

Some weeks have passed. The siege is
raised and about Knoxville the blue skies
overarch a desolate landscape, but the city
streets show signs of resurrection from the
commercial inactivity and gloom which had
for so long enshrouded them. The white
coverings of wagon trains are discernible
creeping toward the town, winding among
the hills and valleys, bringing relief and nu-
cleus of trade ; from their hiding places women and children have sought the shelter of
the houses which the cruelties of the state of
siege have spared. Energies palsied through

a mighty fear are redirected in reopened channels; every shoulder is pressed to the wheel; hope and thankfulness for the few things left, illumine every eye; Knoxville has shaken off her lethargy and taken up again the struggle for life.

In a private ward of a city hospital, Griswold lies hovering between life and death.

His wounds are slowly, very slowly healing. Nothing but his splendid constitution and indomitable will, have kept him from passing to the silent majority. Olmstead is up country, with the battery, but Griswold has good nurses and able doctors who are fighting for him step by step toward recovery.

One night, the train from Chattanooga brought to the shell-riddled town half-a-dozen nurses of the gentler sex; nurses whose presence within the wards raised hopes which were well nigh flagging; women whose patient gentle ministrations found means of soothing many a restless sufferer, whose skill and training supplied the niceties of that art to which men never can attain.

For a day or two Griswold had seemed

to fall back, rather than advance upon
the road to convalescence. At times, his
mind had wandered—Kitty's name had been
often upon his lips and scalding tears had
slowly coursed down his wan, pale cheeks.
Starting from a restless dream one night, a
woman responded to his call and held the
glass to his fevered lips as he quenched his
thirst—then gently smoothed his pillow and
placed her hand upon his brow and pushed
back the disordered hair.

Hugh looked at her long, then turned his
eyes away, and then sought hers again—his
mind was struggling with some image her
face brought back to him. Quietly as she
had come, she moved away again—she read
his trouble but could not answer then, and
her presence only kept him from the sleep he
needed—but the simple gracious act of her
ministration to his need had done its part—
and a few moments later Hugh slept as he
had not slept for days. Night after night
the same noiseless foot-steps moved about the
sick room, supplying the sick man's needs—
little by little the body regained its strength

—little by little the wandering mind fastened its hold upon familiar things. At last, one night, as the doctor left the ward and those preparations for the long hours before day—the shaded light, the smoothing of the pillows, the sleeping draught, the hundred little things a woman's tact suggests—were all completed, Hugh beckoned the nurse to his bedside. For a moment he looked up into her face as though doubtful of himself, but only for an instant.

"Madelaine," he said, "you here?"

"Yes, and glad to be here; but you must not talk; there will be time enough by and by—sleep now," she answered, and she moved away a little and watched him as his eyes slowly closed and a look of quiet content spread over his face and the sleep of rejuvenation took possession of him, and seating herself beside the table, upon which a little clock ticked busily, the sweet gentle woman thanked God in her heart that her coming had borne good fruit, and began the lonely vigil of the night.

Days had passed into weeks; Griswold is

up and about again. The chill has melted
from out the sky and the soft Southern air
is astir and busied with its work of bedeck-
ing the hill-sides with fragrant bloom—everywhere the unsightly evidences of hostile
presence are fading before the march of re-
generation—the city is taking on its old life
again—the farmer is busy with his fields.
Madelaine and Griswold, sitting upon the
verandah outside the latter's room, looking
out into the light of the dying day, watching
the pretty river in its flow, on past the city,
through the distant meadows and the
stretches of pines and walnut which hemmed
them in; below them a little steamer, busy
with preparations for departure, and the
murmur of the city's life borne faintly to
their ears,

Conscious that between them, now that
Hugh is beyond the need of nursing, has
arisen a singular sense of embarrassment,
and Hugh, who to-morrow will be starting
for the East, feels that he cannot go before
pouring out to Madelaine the full measure
of his heartfelt gratitude for that care and

tenderness which he had so sadly needed and she so willingly had bestowed. Turning to her he took her hand in his and pressed it to his lips as he said :

" Madelaine, how can I speak to a heart so kind and true as yours in words which shall tell you all the gratitude which moves my own. You have given me my life, Madelaine, for I doubt if less careful nursing could have availed against what seemed the herald of the end, but what can I return to you? The iron of bitterness has eaten into my soul, passion is dead within me ; I but stand above the grave which has swallowed up that which, in its birth, its beauty, and its sweetness, brought my earthly heritage of joy, and in its death left me the legacy of loneliness and despair. You and I, Madelaine, have both had rude and hard awakenings; let us, in our sorrow, join the hands of friendship, and as down life's vista we move, seeking for that avenue whose sign-post shall mark the turning-point from our earthly pilgrimage, pause, and say there the last farewell which life allows, proud in our loyalty to our beloved dead, true in our friendship for each other."

And so they parted, and Madelaine from her window that night looked out upon the silver thread of water on which she could hear the beat of the little steamer's life, and thought how sweet it was to feel that beneath God's skies there beat so true a heart as Hugh's, and that *she* could proudly call him—friend. But some things yield to Time's conquering power, and so at last the signs of war faded from the land, and the healing influences of purer thought and kindlier impulse developed fairer scenes, and where before ten thousand men had stood in angry mood, now flowed the peaceful tide of husbandry, and flowers blossomed and song birds caroled their sweetest lays, and ugly scars were smoothed away and the song of " Peace " was afloat upon the air.

" And the stars heard and from their wandering aisles
Dropped down the blessing of their golden smiles."

Marjorie and Olmstead were married a year later, as the purpling vineyards told that the new wine was ready for the gathering. Within sight and sound of the restless waves which washed the white sands bordering a stretch of meadow-land; within the shade of fruit-trees and shelter of vine-clad hills, stood a pretty cottage home, and here *one* woman was returning—beautiful with the influence of a chastening sorrow and the consciousness of sweet charity's work well done—and *another* was departing, the world before her, the star of promise bright in its sphere above; her life aglow, and innocent of the ashes which triumph over hope and follow in the train of disappointment. The sun had hidden his last rays within the engulfing depths of the sea beyond. The sound of "Curfew" came faintly from a distant spire and mingled with the low sweet murmurs of the deep; the shadows deepened—one by one in the vault above, the stars peeped out in emphasis of the reign of night. The bride had said the last farewells to the score of pretty village girls and their lovers, who had flocked in with "Godspeeds" and words of gratulation, and then

Marjorie threw herself into her sister's arms, and wept the bitter tears which ever fall upon the last sweet blossoms growing upon the border-land of girlhood; and Hugh, looking on, took Olmstead by the arm and said to him: " God bless you, boy, and good-by—see to it that the flood of tears which Marjorie is shedding now, following 'the rich, full bound of her heart,' never flows again to the dull accompaniment of a thud."

And Hugh Griswold passed out alone into the night, wending his homeward way along the sands, with which the sea was holding tryst and colloquy and two names the rippling waves kept whispering as he went—Kitty—Madelaine—Kitty—Madelaine—in unwearied iteration till he turned to leave the shore and then, *one* name fell faintly on his ear as some sweet memory of music lingers when the hand has ceased to stir the pulsing string— but the *other* spoke to him from its dwelling place in his heart and on the wind it came to him borne from *her* resting place upon the hill above the rushing river.

THE END.